Was Raine dreaming?

Raine couldn't believe this was happening. Not to her. Not now. Weak-kneed, she melted against him, lost for a moment in the wonder of his kiss, all too aware of the day her heart thundered against his as she threaded her fingers into his rich, curly hair. She wanted the moment to go on forever.

Any doubts she'd had before coming here evaporated with his touch. She would never love anyone in the world the way she loved Alan Decker.

It would make saying goodbye to him ten thousand times harder. But she had a promise to keep.

A tear escaped from the corner of her lashes.

SALLY LAITY is an accomplished writer of both contemporary and historical romances and has firmly established herself in the inspirational romance field. Her most recent novels include *Second Spring* and *The Kiss Goodbye*.

To Mom with love . . .
I think you would have liked this one.

I would like to thank my critique group—Dianna Crawford, Jo Frazier, and Sue Rich—for all the help during the writing of this book. And a special thanks to my friend, Ramona Stewart, for supplying me with current information on Rocky Mountain House, Alberta, where I spent a most treasured year of my life.

Books by Sally Laity

ROMANCE READER—TWO BOOKS IN ONE

RR10—Second Spring & The Kiss Goodbye

Don't miss out on any of our super romances. Write to us at the following address for information on our newest releases and club information.

Heartsong Presents Reader's Service
P.O. Box 719
Uhrichsville, OH 44683

Reflections of the Heart

Sally Laity

Heartsong Presents

My world was once a solitary place . . .
    Bland and colorless.
I thought it would always remain so,
    Until you came into my life
    With your laughter and joy.
You brought radiance, and hope,
    And all around me were shades of love . . .
        An endless rainbow of subtle hues.
How can I thank you for showing me
    That solitude is only emptiness
        in disguise.
    That hope restored gives new life,
        and more.
How can I tell you
    Of the beauty in your soul,
    Of how you look beyond imperfections
        to find something of worth . . .
    And how I live again
        Because of you.

ISBN 1-55748-325-6

Reflections of the Heart

Unless otherwise identified, scripture texts are from the
Holy Bible, New International Version,
copyright © 1973, 1978, 1984 International Bible Society.
Used by permission of Zondervan Bible Publishers.

All of the characters and events in this book are fictitious.
Any resemblance to actual persons, living or dead, or to actual events is purely coincidental.

PRINTED IN U.S.A.

one

As water reflects a face, so a man's heart
reflects the man.   Proverbs 27:19

At least the echoes were gone now. Sounds no longer
reverberated through the big, L-shaped farmhouse since
the furniture had been unshrouded and moved back into
the proper places.

Shirring the new valance onto the curtain rod, Raine
Montrose paused and gazed through the dining room window
at the picturesque quarter-section of land that had been willed
to her father upon his only brother's death two years ago.
Nestled in the rolling hills and meadows of rural Rocky
Mountain House, Alberta, the setting was breathtaking.
Across the gravel road on the rise fifty yards to the north,
bright autumn golds and yellows already blazed among the
spruce and tamarack on the hill, a palette which was repeated
in the trees and bushes dotting Misty Hills Ranch.

"Not much like Haiti, is it?" her father, Lucas Montrose,
said from the next room.

Raine smiled over her shoulder, then continued working. "No. Mama would've really loved it here." The
thought brought a sharp stab of grief.

"That she would. She always did love southern Alberta."

And she should have lived to come back to it. Raine thought
bitterly. After serving the Lord all those years in that tiny
clinic, there should have been a time for Mama to enjoy life.
One thing was certain: Raine had no intention of making the
same mistake. She'd follow her own dreams now. "There.
How's that?" she said a little too brightly as she climbed

5

down from the stool and stepped back.

Standing in the squared archway of the adjoining sitting room, her dad cocked his graying head and nudged his glasses into place with a knuckle. "Not bad. Not bad at all." Turning back to his own chore, he removed three more books from a carton on the floor and put them with others already on the bookshelf against the paneled south wall.

Raine watched his slow movements with a twinge of sadness, then folded the step stool and eyed the airy voile curtains she had just hung. The delicate hue of the embroidered flower sprays matched exactly the clear blue of Alberta's late September sky and made a refreshing change from the drab chintz she'd replaced.

Moving again to the window, she pushed a lock of red-gold hair away from her eyes and peered outside. She looked with critical appraisal at the property which in the three weeks since their arrival had already come to feel like home. Even in its present state of disrepair, Misty Hills would return to its former glory with a bit of good hard work.

Raine's father moved to her side. "You were only a little girl last time we were here, remember?"

"I was six," she said wistfully. "And Mark was ten. We loved that summer here with Uncle Sheldon and Aunt Violet." *When we all were young and healthy*, her mind added. Raine cast a glance at her father. The loss of Mama, coupled with a recent illness, had robbed his complexion of its normally robust glow and left him looking frail. He'd lost weight, and even the new slacks he'd bought hung on his scant frame. Window light illuminated a startling increase in silver strands throughout his thinning, once-brown hair. Raine blinked back threatening tears.

"Sure was a time to remember," her father recalled. "One

of the best furloughs we ever had. Sheldon was in his element running this little ranch, breeding that small herd of exotic cattle as he'd always dreamed." He expelled a slow breath. "Seems strange to be back, now that he's gone. And Violet, too." He paused. "Especially without your mama," he added in a near whisper. "Now they're all with the Lord."

Raine swallowed hard.

In the ensuing silence, a pair of barn swallows swooped low outside the window, then joined others frolicking around the outbuildings. One lit upon the roof of the old barn.

"Daddy," Raine began thoughtfully, "weren't you ever sorry about all the years in Haiti? The thankless work?"

He turned steady blue eyes her way. "I never thought of it as thankless, hon. Not for a minute. Don't you ever think it, either. The only lasting happiness there is in this life comes from being where the Lord calls you."

Well, He never called *me* there, she wanted to say. She was glad they'd finally left that place. If they'd come to Canada even a year ago, Mama would never have caught that fever. She'd still be alive. And her father wouldn't look quite so haggard, either. With a determined shrug of her shoulders, Raine tucked her pink cotton blouse tighter into the waistband of her jeans and forced a smile. "Well, what do you say we take a break?"

"Splendid. Both of us could use one."

As they relaxed at the handmade dining table Sheldon Montrose had fashioned years ago in his workshop, Raine offered a plate of blueberry muffins to her father, then helped herself while he poured steaming tea into two mugs.

A loud racket carried from the gravel road north of the farm, and they both looked up as a powerful truck rumbled by, a full load of cut trees strapped to its long-bed trailer. Clouds of dust roiled into the air.

"My goodness," Raine said. "What would happen if something were to get in its way?"

"Most folks are probably used to those by now, I'd imagine. They probably don't even take notice."

"All the same, we'd better keep an eye out when we go up on that road—even just to the mailbox."

That afternoon while her father rested in his bedroom, Raine decided to explore the surrounding countryside. She pulled a gray sweatshirt over her blouse and slipped on some leather boots. Taking a sketch pad and drawing case from the desk in the sitting room, she packed her tote bag and slung the strap over her shoulder.

After a quick trip to the mailbox, Raine came back with two letters. The one to her father from her older brother, Mark, she set just inside the door for her return. The other, from her best friend, she took along.

Storm and Buckwheat, the last of Uncle Sheldon's saddle horses, pranced toward Raine as she approached. She was glad Mr. Wilcox from the next farm to the west had looked after the animals until she and her father had arrived.

"Hi, you two," she crooned, offering each a lump of sugar from her pocket. She stroked their velvet muzzles. "How're you doing, huh?"

The smaller of the pair, Storm, a striking black and white pinto with a black mane and tail, pressed against Raine with his nose.

She giggled. "Lonesome, are you? Well, I've come to take you for a ride. How about that?" After saddling the horse, she led him out of the corral and mounted, nudging him out of the main gate.

A narrow dirt road cut from the main gravel route above

their property and sloped ever so gently downward toward thick forest to the south. A mild breeze stirred the trees lined on either side. Overhead a jet parted the blue of the sky with a feathery trail of white.

The rural area surrounding the town of Rocky Mountain House certainly looked different from the place where she'd grown up, she decided. Like another world. Lush and thick with a huge variety of trees and bushes, the area was the complete opposite of Haiti, where once glorious stands of mahogany and tropical oak were now only a bygone memory except in the high upper mountain ranges of the country.

Breathing deeply of the cool autumn air, Raine let her eyes wander to a neighboring farm off to her right, where sat a charming gray house with scalloped trim and gabled roof— a far cry, she thought, from the basic wooden structures, thatched shacks and gingerbread dwellings so commonplace in the poor sections on the outskirts of Port-au-Prince. From beside the front door of the farmhouse a dog barked, and a woman tending shrubs lifted a hand in greeting.

Raine returned the wave. This was the life. Neighbors with easy smiles and friendly greetings, instead of often suspicious natives, most of whom were steeped in the dark and fearsome practices of voodoo. It was someone else's turn to help those lost people. Someone else's opportunity to love the children. Determined not to spoil her day with sad remembrances of a special little girl back in Haiti, Raine returned her attention to the present.

A little beyond the last farm the road came to an abrupt end as a silvery blue creek meandered out of the woods. The angle of the afternoon sun sprinkled handfuls of diamonds over the sparkly ripples. A simple concrete and wood bridge spanned the stream, but it apparently knew little use, for the ground immediately across the water showed barely a tire track or foot path.

Raine flung a leg over Storm's back and lowered herself to the ground, fastening the reins around a low tree branch. Taking her drawing things out of the tote bag, she found a comfortable spot on the leaf-strewn ground and opened to a clean sheet in the tablet.

The momentarily forgotten letter tumbled into Raine's lap. She picked it up and tore it open, unfolding the pages written in her best friend, Sarah Hamilton's, neat hand:

> *Hi, You,*
>
> *Boy, it seems a hundred years since you left me behind! As they say, I miss your smiley face. It's dreadful to get up every morning and go by myself to the clinic, and the days are ever so long.*
>
> *Danielle still asks after you. She can't understand why you're not around anymore. I barely have time to hold her and read stories the way you always did, but I try. I found her crying behind the supply shed yesterday, so I picked her up and took her home, assuring her you missed her too, that you still think about her and love her. I don't imagine anyone could forget that sweetheart.*

Raine swallowed a lump in her throat at the thought of the little bronze-skinned imp with huge black eyes who had shadowed her and Sarah day and night whenever they were on hiatus from school. One of eight children in a family, Dani knew neglect and indifference. Poverty and hunger had already taken a toll on her fragile body. She reveled in the attention the two older girls had showered upon her. It had

been hard to leave her behind. With a sigh, Raine looked back
to the text:

> *Mark and Ruth look happy together. Mark has built*
> *a little place of their own within walking distance of the*
> *clinic. I wouldn't be surprised if Ruthie's expecting,*
> *from the way she's glowing all the time. It couldn't be*
> *just love, could it?*
>
> *Everybody asks after you. Perhaps we really are*
> *appreciated here, after all. There's been a new out-*
> *break of fever in the next village, so we sure keep busy.*
>
> *Thanks awfully for the invitation, by the way. I asked*
> *Dad if perhaps I might come for a visit, and he's*
> *considering it. Sure would be great to get away for*
> *awhile—and see you. In the meantime, don't forget me.*
> *Trust things are well with your father. Write soon.*
>
> > *Love 'n stuff,*
> > *Me*

Leaning back against a poplar tree, Raine fought against
melancholy. She refused to feel homesick for that country
which had cost her mother's life, taken her before her time.
Realizing she was crumpling Sarah's letter, Raine quickly
smoothed it out and tried to force aside her resentment.

She envisioned her blonde and bubbly friend whose
sparkly gray eyes would gleam with mischievous plans for
another school prank. Despite occasional rough spots over
the years, they'd had their share of fun growing up. Raine
could barely remember what life had been like before she and
the British girl met. Living next door to one another at the
compound, they had grown up together while their parents
worked at a tiny medical facility on the outer fringe of Port-

au-Prince. Early on, watching all the suffering around them, they had made a pact to leave Haiti for good the first chance either of them got. Raine's chance had come the hard way. But maybe Sarah's wouldn't be far behind.

Folding the missive, she put it inside the bag and concentrated on blocking in the components of the scene. Then she relaxed and crossed her ankles, enjoying the rustle of the wind through the trees as she shaded in the background of the sketch. Someday soon she would explore along the creek in both directions and find out where it came from. where it went. But not just yet. Not while her dad looked so poorly. She didn't want to leave him alone too long. She tucked her charcoal pencil over her ear and yawned, stretching a kink out of her back.

A bright glint of sunshine sparkled from a clearing not far beyond her position. Raine straightened, squinting to focus her vision in that direction.

A secluded cabin nestled snugly in the dappled shade. Constructed of dark logs chinked with white, the structure had white sills and red shutters. Framed by evergreen boughs, as it was from Raine's position, it made a charming scene. She studied the neat roofline and tidy front porch.

A second spark of sunshine twinkled, then a third, as a stained glass sun catcher twirled on a string above the banister. She smiled to herself. Putting her sketchbook aside, she stood and brushed off her backside, then leaned down to retrieve her things. Ignoring the bridge she stepped cautiously from stone to stone across the shallows, moving a few yards nearer the dwelling. Then she sat down on a log and turned to the next page.

A loud bark shattered the silence. A blur of russet flashed into the edge of her vision as a huge Irish setter charged toward her.

Heart pounding, Raine gasped and jumped to her feet, spilling her belongings. She flattened her back against the nearest tree and shielded herself with her arms. Eyes closed, she braced herself for the dog's lunge. Its fangs.

Someone whistled, and the padded footfalls stopped.

Raine released a shuddering breath. The animal was someone's pet. She lifted her lashes a fraction.

The setter, though still merely a few feet away, no longer appeared threatening. Still panting from the run, it turned and loped away toward a man who appeared to be returning to the cabin from the woods beyond.

Raine's pulse slowed to normal. She looked more closely at the stranger.

Quite tall and thin, he wore faded jeans, a blue plaid shirt, and a black, wide-brimmed, western hat which made his eyes appear little more than dark slits within its shadow. A hunting rifle hung behind one shoulder.

She smiled nonchalantly and waved. "Hi."

The man lifted his chin a notch and stared, then swung toward the porch. With his head he gave a curt signal to the dog, who followed his master obediently up the slate-gray steps and into the cabin. The door closed behind them.

How rude! Raine thought, staring after them. He hadn't so much as waved or tried to be the least neighborly. Must be the local grouch. But whoever he was, he was no concern of hers. It was getting late. She'd best hurry home before Daddy started to worry.

She retrieved her strewn art supplies, then walked back to where the pinto grazed on the tall grass beside the stream. Mounting, she cast a last glance toward the little house, but it was now blocked from view by trees. She sniffed in derision. Its anything-but-neighborly occupant had already used up more than his deserved share of her consideration. Banishing further thought of him, she turned the horse purposely up the lane to the open, split-rail gate of home.

After seeing to the horses' needs, Raine found her father puttering in the greenhouse, a once-efficient structure Uncle Sheldon had built on the south end of the enclosed breezeway which connected the house to his workshop.

Raine's father looked up as she entered, his pasty complexion evident in the waning light.

"Oh, hi, Daddy. Have I been gone too long?"

"No, not at all. You need time for yourself."

Stepping on the envelope she'd forgotten about, she picked it up, then crossed the flagstone floor to his side. "What are you doing?"

"Just checking things out. The soil feels so rich." He spilled some dirt from an upraised palm and chuckled in wonder. "Remember those pathetic, anemic vegetables we eked out of the overused plot next to our house?"

"Who could forget? They seemed great at the time."

"I suppose." Her father pressed a button, and electrically controlled slats squeaked upward on aluminum tracks and covered the glass canopy. "Needs a bit of oil or something. but doesn't this beat all? There's even a watering system. Turns on over there on the end, only the knob's missing."

Raine shook her head. "Guess Uncle Sheldon thought the growing season was too short in Canada. Maybe I'll pick up some seeds when I go into town. By the way, a letter came today. From Mark." She held it out until he took it.

"Good. He's been weighing on my mind lately. I wonder how his doctoring's coming along."

"Sarah says he's doing okay. I heard from her, too. She

asked after you."

The following morning dawned magnificently, sporting an abundance of puffy, strawberry pink clouds against a clear blue sky. From the Wilcox farm, the sound of a rooster crowing carried on the western breeze.

Raine stood at her window in her thin batiste nightie, elbows resting against the sill as she gazed outside. She breathed a habitual prayer of thanks. Tugging on some jeans and a pullover, she went outside to tend the horses.

Later, as she towel-dried her red-gold hair and combed out the flowing waves, she could hear her father stirring in his room. She hurried out to start coffee and pancakes. Already she'd gotten used to the incredible conveniences of reliable electricity and a real stove with an oven. She'd even found herself beginning to enjoy cooking as she experimented with Aunt Violet's vast collection of recipes.

"Morning," her father said, coming to the table. Hair still damp from his shower and slicked back, he looked quite rested and more like his old self.

"Morning, Daddy. Pretty one, isn't it?" Raine flipped the pancakes onto two plates and carried them to the table, placing them beside the butter and warm maple syrup. "Thought I'd ride into town later. Is there anything besides seeds you'd like me to bring back for you?" Taking her seat, she reached for the coffee pot and filled their cups.

"Any bookstores in Rocky?"

"I didn't notice any last time I was there, but I'll ask."

He reached for her hand, then bowed his head for grace. "We thank You, dear Lord, for this lovely day and for Your bountiful goodness to us. We're humbled in the provision of this wonderful home. We are truly blessed. And we thank You for our food. Bless it, Lord. May we be ever faithful in seeking to do Your will. In Jesus' name, Amen."

"Amen," Raine echoed. What more could there be for them to do? Hadn't they already served the Lord years and years? She poured syrup over her pancakes and made an effort to sound casual. "Got a special book in mind?"

"No. Whatever looks good. The days seem so . . . long. You know." With a sigh, he took a sip of coffee, then set down the cup.

Raine stroked his gnarled hand. "I know. I miss Mama, too. She'd have been in her glory here, don't you think?"

"Yes. If only . . . ." His blue eyes misted over, and he shifted on the chair and cleared his throat. "Remember how she missed seein' big trees? 'Real ones,' as she called them, not just royal palms and the like."

Raine nodded and cut into her flapjacks.

"Must be more around here than anyplace I've been. I met her in a grove of trees, you know," he said absently.

"Oh?" At his mellow expression, she quieted. Time for telling stories had been scarce on the mission field.

He lifted a chunk of pancake to his mouth, chewing slowly before he swallowed. "Prettiest little thing I ever laid eyes on, she was. About sixteen. Swinging on this big long swing her pa had put up for her on the edge of their place." A pensive smile drew up one corner of his mouth. "She looked up at me and smiled, and it was just like sunshine coming out after the rain. Couldn't take my eyes off that pretty red hair of hers. I loved the way the sun set it afire, like spun gold. It looked so silky. Was, too. Always did love the feel of her hair. It was a lot like yours," he said, ruffling Raine's shoulder-length waves. "And your eyes are the same shade of green. Sometimes when I look at you . . . ." His words trailed off with a sigh.

Raine smiled, recalling the natural beauty of her mother's peaches-and-cream face, the pleasant, melodic voice that had been forever silenced earlier that year. Her passing had left a hole in Raine's life, one she doubted would ever be filled again. But certain that her father needed her to be strong, she kept her sorrow inside, not wanting to add to his burden.

Her dad lowered his gaze and rubbed a hand across his mouth. "Knew right then I'd marry her. Took us awhile to convince your grandma and grandpa Palmer, though, with me being eight years older than their daughter. But they finally gave in, and we married soon as she graduated from nursing school. Never regretted it for a minute." He paused. "Sometimes, though, I wonder if I might've given her a better life. One without so much hardship. Maybe I shouldn't have taken her off to a dark place like Haiti."

Raine reached over and squeezed his forearm. It still felt firm and comforting beneath her fingers. "Don't feel that way, Daddy. Mama was really happy. Being with you was all she wanted. I never heard her complain."

He smiled gratefully.

A few moments passed before he spoke again. "Thought I might take a little walk around the property later. Been so long since I was here."

Main Street in the rustic town of Rocky Mountain House had a moderate amount of mid-afternoon traffic moving among its few dozen, assorted-sized business establishments as Raine rode down the main thorough-fare. After tying Storm's reins to a light pole, she entered the I.G.A. with her grocery list.

Molly Griffith, a clerk Raine had met her first day in town, looked up with a smile that wrinkled the round pink nose on her plump face as she put down the feather duster she held. "How do, young lady. Gettin' settled in at the old Montrose place, are ya'?" Brushing off her hands, she straightened the collar of her long-sleeved, knit blouse.

"Yes, thanks. Nice to see you again. We just need a few supplies. Mind if I look around?"

"Not a'tall. Take your time." Grasping the handle of the duster again, she flicked it over her register and the attached counter as a customer loaded items from a shopping cart onto the moving belt.

Raine gathered the groceries she needed and headed for Mrs. Griffith's till, where the items were rung up.

"Will we be seein' ya' at church this week?" the woman asked, placing change into Raine's palm, then bagging the small order.

"Not yet, I'm afraid. My father's still not quite himself. But I'm sure he'll start perking up now that he has a place where he can putter around."

"Mm. No shortage of things to fix on a spread that's sat empty for a spell, that's for sure." The woman's ample bosom rose and fell with her breathing as she smiled good-naturedly and handed over the bag. "Well, we'll be sayin' a prayer for him, then." The skin beside her twinkly blue eyes crinkled with her grin as she tucked a few wisps of permed brownish hair behind one ear.

"Thanks. He'll be glad to hear there are so many friendly people in town." Raine turned to leave, then stopped. "Would there happen to be a bookstore around, Mrs. Griffith? Maybe even a Christian one?"

"Oh, call me Molly. No need to be formal, child. An' yes," she said, moving to the window and pointing a pudgy finger to indicate the direction. "The Bible and Book Nook's thataway. They carry most ever'thing you might want."

"Thanks again. See you in a few days, then, Molly."

Browsing among the heavily laden shelves in the bookstore, Raine took longer than she'd planned in choosing a missionary biography for her father. Then she picked up a novel for herself. The atmosphere was so warm and friendly she wished she had more time to check out the music tapes and other things, but that would have to wait for another time. Making her way to the counter, she paid for the books.

Outside, Raine divided her purchases into canvas bags on either side of Storm's saddle, then mounted the horse and guided him along the edge of the road.

Halfway home she heard a vehicle approaching in the distance, the first she had seen along the way. Noting absently how new and shiny the brown metallic Ford Bronco looked as it passed, she gave a friendly wave.

But the driver didn't acknowledge it. He merely ducked his head lower beneath the wide black brim of his hat and drove on. The sight of the Irish setter in the passenger seat came as no surprise.

"Have a nice day," Raine said sarcastically, glaring after the vehicle as swirling dust clogged her throat.

That man could use some manners, that was for sure. Someone needed to put him in his place—and the sooner the better. She nudged Storm's flanks, and he picked up the pace.

two

The next few weeks turned gradually cooler and brought a few days of intermittent heavy showers reminiscent of Haiti's rainy season. Water pelted the roof of the house and streamed down the awning above the dining room window into a growing puddle below. The horses hunched together in the wetness, bedraggled manes plastered to their necks.

Raine turned from the sight and studied the great stone fireplace which dominated the north wall of the sitting room. Surely it must be functional, she thought. Putting on a sweater, she went out to Uncle Sheldon's workshop, where she had discovered earlier an abundant supply of split logs. She filled her arms with wood and went inside.

After wadding up some old newspapers around the wood on the grate, Raine struck a match to them. They caught fire at once. But within seconds, clouds of black smoke billowed into the room, and the smoke detector on the far wall sounded a shrill alarm.

"What's going on?" Dad asked, coming out of the bathroom in his plaid flannel robe.

"I . . . I think I set the house on fire! I'd better call the fire department."

"Wait, hon. Did you open the damper?"

"The what?" she yelled above the din.

With a tolerant laugh, Raine's father squeezed her shoulder, then went over to the alarm. The blaring noise stopped abruptly as he disconnected the wire. "You open the doors and windows. I'll take care of the rest."

As Raine followed his orders, she watched her father open

the fire screen and use a piece of wood to push at something above the burning logs. It creaked open, and almost at once the smoke began to rise up the chimney.

She met his twinkling blue eyes with chagrin. "Sorry, Daddy. Guess I have a lot to learn about living in a cold climate, huh?"

He padded across the room in his corduroy slippers and put an arm about her. "Oh, it seems to me I had to learn the same lesson once in my life, as I recall."

"But not when you were twenty-three years old, I'll bet."

"Well, no. More like seven. But at least it's not one we soon forget. Come on over here, and I'll show you the handle to the damper."

After a filling breakfast of scrambled eggs and bacon, Raine and her father carried mugs of coffee in by the fire.

"This will probably be our favorite spot, come winter," Raine said, sitting on one end of the settee upholstered in ivory and shades of gray.

Lucas nodded and took the other side. "No doubt we'll find out why Shel put in such a big hearth." He assessed the fine workmanship and the carved wood mantel, then let his gaze rove over the knotty pine paneling which had been used exclusively throughout the house. His brother had put the functional workshop and the incredible assortment of tools and power equipment to good use over the years. Every chair and table in the place had been fashioned by his skillful hand, wonderfully sturdy and expertly finished. Propping a foot on the coffee table, Lucas relaxed and studied his daughter.

Raine had seemed happy enough since they had come to the ranch. Yet she'd been unusually quiet, and the customary light was absent from her eyes. He watched orange flames flicker against the glazed green depths as she stared unseeing toward the fire. "I unpacked your Bible the other day," he said quietly. "Set it on the bookcase, in case you were looking for it."

She blinked. "Oh. Thanks."

Lucas decided not to mention the fine coating of dust gathering on its burgundy cowhide cover. Had she even missed it? He couldn't remember the last time he'd seen her with it, though he knew it had been her practice to read through her Bible every year. And she no longer volunteered to pray even at mealtime. He took a sip, then set his cup down. "I always did like the pine paneling here."

"Hm? Oh, yes. It's nice." She glanced around. "I wish he'd have made one or two rooms different, though."

"What do you mean?"

"Well, you know. Variety's supposed to be the spice of life, and all that. Sometimes I feel like all the knots in the walls are looking at me."

He smiled. "Well, it's your house now. Why don't you do something about it?"

She looked at him. "Like what?"

"I don't know. Paint your bedroom. Fix it the way you'd like it. Paper a wall in the kitchen."

A smile brightened her expression. "I don't know how to wallpaper."

"I do. I can help you."

She rose and picked up their empty cups, then carried them to the sink. On her way back, she stopped in the archway and turned toward the kitchen.

Lucas watched Raine perusing the room, her head tipped in thought. He could almost see the workings of her nimble mind, measuring, assessing possibilities. How long had that deep sadness been in those wide green eyes of hers? He'd been so taken up with trying to live without his dear Helen, he'd never taken time to notice that their daughter had some pain of her own to work through. Perhaps a good project would be just the thing she needed now.

The next afternoon, Raine put the paint roller she'd been using back in the tray and wiped her hands on some paper towels. Pushing her bed close as possible to the bone-white wall, she straightened the multi-hued floral coverlet and fluffed the pillow in its ruffled sham. A sudden warm shaft of sunshine poured through the parted sheer curtains, and she stepped to look out. Everything sparkled glorious and clean, and just outside her room the huge pine dripped water from its needles. The sky off to the west was a cloudless cerulean blue. Thoughts of getting back to work on her drawings cheered her as she carried the paint supplies out to the workshop.

"Finished already?" Dad asked upon her return.

Raine nodded. "But no peeking till it's dry." She paused. "Thought I'd take an hour and work on my sketches down at the creek—unless there's something you need me to do."

"No. We've been cooped up for days. You go on. I'm fine."

She crossed to him and gave a peck on his cheek, then plucked her hooded sweatshirt from the rack by the door. "Good. I won't be too long."

As she saddled the pinto and rode to her favorite spot, Raine determined to finish only the drawing of the stream. After all, she reminded herself as she secured Storm's reins, the cabin which she'd found so incredibly interesting a few days before had given her the first bad experience she'd had since she'd come to Alberta. Why tempt fate?

But her eyes kept wandering beyond the trees to the little

clearing. And more than once she caught herself not even working at all as her curiosity intensified. Finally, unable to stifle it any longer, she stood and peered on tiptoe toward the log structure, wondering if its strange occupant was home.

Perhaps she could go quietly over there and finish at least the basic sketch without being noticed—if that hairy red beast were otherwise occupied. It was worth a try, in any event. Not taking her eyes from the cabin, Raine bent and picked up her things.

Since the rainfall, the creek flowed faster, tumbling and gurgling over the myriad rocks beneath the surface. Raine crossed the bridge to the other side, then chose a dry seat on a low branch facing the little house. For several moments she just stared. What if the man saw her? What if the dog were loose and the owner couldn't prevent another attack?

With little hesitation, Raine made up her mind. She'd go over to the cabin, knock on the door, and . . . and . . . Well, she only wanted to finish a sketch, after all. No harm in that. Surely he couldn't have a problem with something so simple. Before she talked herself out of it, she put the plan into motion.

The bottom porch step squeaked under her foot.

Instantly from inside, the dog barked. Once. Twice.

Raine swallowed. She wished she hadn't come. The dog might charge right past its master and go for her throat. "Don't be such a dope," she muttered under her breath. Taking a deep breath to fortify herself, she went purposely up the remaining steps and knocked on the door.

It opened just a crack. At least a good head taller than she, the dark stranger stood towering above her, unspeaking, unsmiling. A light brown eye assessed her from the ground up in a second. The vee of a frown appeared over the bridge of his long straight nose.

Raine moistened her lips, willing her voice to come out naturally. "Hi," she croaked, then cleared her throat and tried again. "Sorry to bother you. I'm Raine Montrose—from Misty Hills." She pointed in the general direction of the farm. "I'm not here to bother you, or anything, I'm just doing a few sketches in the area and need to finish the ones I've already started—" she barely gulped a breath, "if you and your dog don't mind, of course."

The man grimaced, regarding her coolly. "I'll keep him in," he said flatly, then closed the door.

Hmph, Raine thought. *Nice to meet you, too*. "Thanks," she said in a bright enough voice to carry inside. Going down the steps again, she returned to her vantage point and picked up her tablet, opening it to the page on which she'd begun the cabin. Working quickly as possible, she put in as much detail as she could amidst the eerie feeling that he watched her from behind one of his darkened windows.

Later that night in bed, she withdrew one arm from under the covers and crooked it under her head. Bright moonlight illuminated the pink ruffled priscillas at the window and shone through the transparent fabric, glowing over the spread and freshly painted walls.

Raine hadn't been able to get thoughts of *that man* out of her mind. At the ridiculous thought of him peering through an inch of open door space, she smiled and shook her head. What on earth would make someone so—what? Suspicious? Leery of strangers? She felt his eyes upon her even yet, as though he still watched.

Alan Decker locked the front and back doors of his cabin out of habit and went into his bedroom, where he dressed for bed, then turned down the covers on the big four-poster. After slipping between the cool sheets, he turned off the lamp and stared in the semi-darkness at the open-beamed ceiling. Cool, crisp night air billowed the plaid curtains at the window, making the brass rings dance as they tugged against the rod. Faraway he heard the lonely cry of a wolf.

Dek's mouth curled at one side with disdain. Rain, that little wisp of a girl had said her name was. Probably some second-generation hippie with sisters called Cloud and Flower, and a brother named Waterfall. And she fancied herself some sort of an artist. He inhaled long and slow and turned over. He didn't need anyone nosing around. He'd bought this place because of its seclusion. No one ever came by—until Little Miss Montrose, that is. With her titian hair touseled from the wind like a child's, yet something within her sea-green eyes that seemed years older than the rest of her.

He sighed, willing the image from his mind. Oh well, it didn't take long to draw a picture. She'd probably finished it by now. It was highly unlikely she'd be pointing that little freckled nose this way again. Forcing him to hide.

Giving his feather pillow a few sound punches, he nestled into it and closed his eyes.

At the Bible bookstore later that week, Raine picked up a volume of messages by Charles Spurgeon for her dad, and then went by the library. Hoping to find some insight on the reason her drawings appeared flat, she checked out a book on the rudiments of perspective before leaving for home.

When she finally opened the door to the house, the rich aroma of stew wafted toward her. She smiled. It had been awhile since Dad fussed about in the kitchen, though her mom had often confessed that he'd taught her all she knew about cooking. Lately he'd been more like his old self, standing straight, head up, face glowing with purpose, even if his steps still seemed slightly slower than normal. "Daddy?" she called out as she hung her jacket on the coat rack.

"Hi, honey. Sure hope you're hungry. I made enough for the whole town, by the looks of it."

"Smells delicious." Raine entered the kitchen and set down her bag. Reaching inside, she took out one of the books, then held it out to him. "I brought you something."

He wiped his gnarled hands on a towel and took the volume, squinting as he perused the title. "Splendid! I know I'll enjoy that. Thanks." He kissed her cheek and put the book on the counter.

"I'll just wash up and set the table." Hurrying to the bathroom, she ran a comb through the tangled strands of her hair and freshened up. Her cheeks still looked rosy from the cool wind as she washed and dried her hands. She hurried to the dining room, where her father had hastily placed napkins, bowls, and silverware in a pile for her to spread out properly.

He carried the pot into the room and placed it on hot pads in the middle of the table. Then, ladling stew into two bowls, he handed one to her. "While you were gone, Jim Wilcox came by from next door. Offered to drive me over to Red Deer when he goes to pick up some tractor parts he ordered."

"Really?"

He nodded. "I haven't been able to get Shel's old heap running since we've been here. Jim says he knows a fellow who has some decent used cars."

"Great, Dad. It's getting kind of difficult to depend on the horses for all our needs." She buttered a roll and dipped it into her stew.

"I know. About time we're able to go to church and other places."

"The town folks seem really nice. Molly Griffith, at the grocery store, asks about you every time I go there. Did you know the people in her church have been praying for you?"

He chuckled. "No wonder I've been feeling better by the day. I'll have to thank them first time we attend services. Would you pass the butter?"

After handing it to him, Raine watched absently as he liberally coated two warm rolls.

"Daddy?"

Taking a bite, he glanced up.

"Did Mr. Wilcox tell you about any of the neighbors around here?"

"Well," he began. "Let's see. Says the lady down the lane is named Manchester—a widow in her mid-thirties, with three kids. Nobody very close to the east of us. That's about it."

"No mention of anybody . . . unfriendly?"

"No. Why?"

"Oh, I just wondered."

Sitting crosslegged on her bed later that night, Raine opened *Perspective: The Fundamentals* and flipped through the pages, stopping once or twice to examine an illustration which looked interesting. Frowning over one which depicted a block of city buildings receding into infinity, she shook her head. Thank heaven she wouldn't be attempting those. With a sigh she opened to the beginning of the text:

> *Though perspective often is considered frightening, envisioned as a complex web of lines and points obeying some obscure law of mathematics, it's actually just a tool. By it an artist is able to depict three-*

dimensional space on a two-dimensional surface.

The words blurred before Raine's vision as she yawned. Did sketching have to be all that complicated? Deciding it would make more sense in the morning, she set the book on the floor next to the bed and took her Bible from the drawer in the nightstand. It was hopeless to think she'd get back on schedule, so she opened to the book of Psalms and read several, enjoying the poetic style.

During the night, a mist of cold droplets blew across Raine's face, awakening her from a sound sleep. Jumping up, she closed the window, then rubbed the moisture from her upper arms as she stood peering outside. Under the floodlight near the barn, sheets of rain blew in the wind. Alberta certainly had a changeable climate—warm one day, cold the next, then back to warm again. Sunshine for a few hours, then thick clouds. The first week after their arrival the days had started out sunny, but included what seemed like a monsoon every afternoon. She shivered in the night dampness. She had rarely felt cold in Haiti's balmy climate. Even yet she could remember so many tranquil mornings at Port-au-Prince and the way the long arm of the southern peninsula would turn gradually from violet vagueness to green brilliance as the sun rose high in the tropical sky.

Crawling back into bed, Raine pulled the coverlet over her goose pimples and closed her eyes. She wondered if *his* window had been open too, and if he'd had an unexpected shower. Water would probably make that almost-black hair of his even curlier. What a dunce she was becoming, she thought as she shook her head. Especially when she was sleepy. Turning over, she closed her eyes.

In a chair on his front porch, Dek sanded the birdhouse he had finished building the night before. The crack of a twig broke the stillness a handful of yards away, and instantly O'Clancy's head jerked up from his paws.

Dek scanned the area in the direction of the sound and found the source. The willowy redhead. She strolled through the faraway trees, sketch pad under one arm, the reins of Sheldon Montrose's striking pinto in her other hand. Over her denims she wore a canary yellow blouse with rolled up sleeves and there was a navy sweatshirt tied at her waist. She made quite a bright picture among tree trunks still black from the rain. Her shoulder-length hair had been pulled back at the nape of her neck today, he noticed. Not that he cared what she did with it.

What in the world did she find so incredibly fascinating around this place, for Pete's sake? It's not like they lived in the Rockies or on the coast. But he'd seen her everywhere the past several weeks, at the creek, in his own glen, on the road to town, and once even sprawled atop one of the stonewalls lining the lane, drawing in that spiral notebook of hers. Absorbed in her work, she hadn't noticed him. But no matter where he went, *that girl* was forever turning up.

She glanced his way just then and waved.

Dek raked his fingers through his hair with a sigh.

"Hi. How're you doing today?" she yelled. "Some downpour we had last night, huh?"

So she was set on being neighborly. Well, he didn't need neighbors, thanks just the same. He didn't need anybody. Setting down the birdhouse, Dek stood. "C'mon, Clance. Let's go in." He crossed the porch to the door. The dog rose, stretched, then padded along behind him.

"Nice to see you again," came her cheery voice.

Tossing a disbelieving glance over his shoulder at her, Dek lifted his hand in a wave of dismissal—at least he hoped she'd see it as that—then went inside.

Raine tucked her chin and stared. Honestly, she thought. What a jerk. What in the world was wrong with the man? She was only trying to be polite, that's all, not soliciting contributions for the mission. Shaking her head, she angled away from what she assumed was his property and headed toward an appealing stand of birch trees she'd seen a bit farther upstream.

Dek peered out through the edge of a curtain until Little Miss Montrose moved out of his sight. The little fool never carried so much as a .22 with her in all her gallivanting. Didn't she know there were bears around? And wolves? The fact that it was daylight did not rule out the need for some protection in the bush country. What was the matter with her family, anyway, to let a little thing like her run around loose so far from home?

He glanced toward the barn. Knowing he'd probably regret the decision, he let out a resigned breath. Might as well saddle Blackjack and do some hunting for supper. And maybe while he was at it, keep an eye on that stupid female Rembrandt—from a distance.

three

Raine allowed Storm to set his own pace alongside the creek as it meandered through wondrous meadows and thickets. In places the flow widened, spreading out in shimmering shallows which reflected the sky and trees. Then the creek would narrow and deepen into a swifter channel, as if hurrying to find another setting as glorious.

Though the sky was slowly becoming overcast, the temperature remained mild as gray clouds enhanced the play of light and shadow all around. The scent of damp earth carried on cool wind as it ruffled the boughs of lush pines.

Coming upon a spot where a tree had fallen across the stream, Raine stopped and eyed the miniature waterfall with an artist's critical eye. "Hm. Would you look at that," she murmered.

The pinto flicked his ears.

Raine nudged Storm with her knees and guided him through the swift-flowing water to the other side, where higher ground held the possibility of a better angle. But once on top, her eyes caught the sheen of a distant pond glistening through the trees. She urged her mount over the uneven ground toward a scene she had no doubt would be far prettier.

Ringed by dense forest, the small lake seemed to have been placed like a bowl right in the middle of the woods, a setting Raine found peaceful and appealing despite the gloomy sky or the likelihood that even on a sunny day only mid-day rays of sunshine ever touched the area.

She patted Storm's muscled neck. "Let's see what we can find, huh?" Swinging down from the saddle, she took Storm's

reins and led him along the shoreline. When at last she came
to a place where a stand of stately spruce and birch trees cast
their reflections on the water, she tied the horse to a low-
hanging branch.

Raine checked her watch. She should have been home half
an hour ago to start supper, but with the weather as changeable as it had been lately, she decided to take advantage of the
opportunity to be outside. At the very least she could get the
sketch started. She took out her drawing pad and worked for
some time roughing in the background, concentrating on the
composition as her mount grazed nearby.

An odd sound came from partway around the lakeshore,
where Raine had noticed a pair of rustic picnic tables during
her earlier perusal. She closed her book and raised her lashes.

A chill shot through her.

A black bear! Rooting through one of two garbage cans
across the water, the animal poked his snout into a motley
assortment of crumpled bags and trash.

Raine prayed it hadn't seen her yet. She grabbed her things.
Silently, eyes riveted on the hungry beast, she inched her way
backward as her heartbeat throbbed in her ears.

The bear tipped over the can and growled low. Its front
paws groped through the spilled refuse.

Storm's nostrils flared with a faint nervous whinny. He
strained at his tether, forelegs prancing skittishly.

Raine glanced over her shoulder at the horse and saw his
eyes bulging with fear. "Shh, take it easy, boy," she whispered
soothingly, stepping behind the tree and untying the reins.
"We're gonna—" Her fingertips barely brushed the smooth
leather before the pinto yanked free. In a flurry of hoofbeats,
he ran off.

Raine covered her mouth with one hand, barely holding in

a scream as Storm's black tail disappear from view. Terror clawed its way up her spine. Her breaths came in shallow gasps. She peered around a tree trunk toward the garbage cans across the water.

The bear was nowhere.

Oh, Lord, she prayed silently. *Has it gone? Or is it on its way over here? What should I do? Help me*! Her teeth chattered as gooseflesh spread over her entire body. Quietly she kept moving. Her ears tried to catch some indications of the bear's whereabouts, but could hear only the rush of her pounding pulse. She broke into a run. checking over her shoulder every few yards.

Finally, hearing only her own footsteps, Raine slowed to a walk. Thank heaven the creek was just over the rise. Her heartbeat returned to near normal. Breathing a sigh of relief, she emerged from the trees.

The sigh caught in her throat. She searched frantically, fruitlessly for the stream. It had to be here. It had to. She'd come this way, hadn't she? Or perhaps—

Raine spun and looked right. Left. Surely this was the meadow she'd come through earlier. It had to be. But in the fading light it looked like so many others.

A dreadful finality sank like a rock in her heart. She was lost. Tears stung her eyes, and she blinked hard. She must not panic. She'd get through this. Somehow.

Gathering her thoughts in the swiftly fading light, Raine doubted she'd be safe if she remained on the ground. She searched for a sturdy tree. Making her way toward one, she stumbled over a fair-sized stick, then regained her footing. It would make a weapon, at least. She picked it up and threaded it through the back of her belt, then jumped to catch the lowest branch. On the third try she made it. Grasping the limb with all her strength, she threw a leg over and raised herself up. Once on it, she climbed as high as she dared.

Skinning a rabbit on one knee beside his horse, Dek groaned inwardly as the Montrose pinto crashed by him on a straight beam toward home, an empty saddle on its back. Just like he'd figured. Little Miss Artist had gotten herself left behind in the wilds someplace. He had known it would happen sooner or later. It was getting rather late to have to go looking for somebody, and he'd failed once already in the hero department, he reminded himself bitterly. He emptied his lungs in resignation.

Dek dropped his intended supper and sheathed his Buck knife, then rinsed his hands in the creek and wiped them on his handkerchief. "C'mon, Clance," he said as he mounted Blackjack. "Let's get going."

The setter plunged playfully ahead, a dark splotch of flying fur, as Dek set out to find the Montrose girl. So far she'd pretty well stuck to the creek, at least. He'd follow that for awhile.

Raine shivered in the growing darkness. She zipped her sweatshirt all the way to her throat, then clutched the cold branch tighter. How could she have been so stupid? She'd never stayed out after supper before. Dad must be out of his mind with worry. And now she'd even lost the horse. He'd taken off like his hooves were on fire, and was probably half way to British Colombia by now—or Saskatchewan. She had no idea where the compass points were.

An owl hooted, the lonely sound coming from eerily close by.

Somewhere in the distance she heard the unmistakable yipping of coyotes. It gave her the creeps, and she shuddered, clutching the branch so hard her hands hurt. Coyotes couldn't climb trees. Hopefully.

She released a shuddering breath. "Help! Somebody! Can anyone hear me?"

The blackness around her took on hairy shapes as she imagined wild creatures catching her scent, pawing the ground beneath her. Drooling.

"Help!" Raine called again. She had passed only one house on her way, and it had appeared deserted. No one would hear her. Unable to stop the tears that brimmed in her eyes, she felt the warmth of the first two course down her cold cheeks. *Stop it*, she told herself. *Don't give in. Didn't it say in the Bible, "I will trust and not be afraid?"* Sure, she'd read it a hundred times. But there was that other verse, too: "When I am afraid, I will trust in You." "Dear God, are you there?" Rained asked in the growing darkness. "I'm so afraid."

Dek reined Blackjack to a stop and listened. He thought he'd heard a voice.

Clancy bounded away from the stream and raced into the woods like he knew where he was going. Dek followed.

Soon enough, Dek heard the dog's excited yelps. And a woman's screams. Nearing the site, Dek could make out Clancy standing with his forepaws on the broad trunk of a tree, barking upward into branches outlined against the night sky. He guided his mount toward it.

"Go away! Go away! Help me, somebody!" came a voice pitched high with terror.

Dek chuckled wryly, then gave a quick whistle. The dog ceased its noise. "Miss Montrose?"

Raine felt the greatest relief she had ever known in her entire life. That wasn't a coyote trying to claw its way up to her. For the first time in several minutes she opened her tightly clenched eyes and peered down. "Y . . . yes."

"Thought you might need a ride home."

Recognition of the voice diminished her relief by half. She swallowed. Not that she was particular, exactly, but of all the people in the world who might have been sent by God to rescue her, why did it have to be someone who already couldn't abide her? That man probably thought she was a first class idiot now. With supreme effort she eased her death-hold on the limb in front of her.

"We've about run out of light," he said obligingly. "Think you could come down in the near future?"

She complied, moving with as much poise as she could muster, being stiff from maintaining one position for so long. Reaching the bottom limb, she swung down and dropped to the ground with a thud. She placed her hands in her pockets and raised a self-conscious gaze, hoping she didn't glow like a neon light from embarrassment. She couldn't make out the man's face tucked into the shadow of his hat brim, but knew he had to be mocking her. "I . . . was afraid of wild animals," she said meekly.

Dek scooted back in the saddle, then reached down and pulled her up effortlessly, seating her in front of himself. He turned his black horse and nudged him toward the Montrose place, while Clancy scampered ahead. He could tell the girl was on the verge of falling apart. Her head was bowed slightly, and she was trembling.

"What in the world kind of name is Rain?" he asked, trying to put her at ease. "Are you a leftover flower child, or something?"

She sniffed. "It's a nickname. Short for Lorraine. My dad started calling me that when I was little. It has an 'e' on the end."

"Oh."

"What's yours?"

"Dek. Short for Decker. Alan Decker. I drop the 'c.' " Why on earth he'd added that, he had no idea.

"It's . . . different."

"Yeah, well, a darn sight better than being called Al."

A chunk of silence hung heavy as the horse plodded along.

"I was at a pond," she finally said. "Th . . . there was a bear. My horse—"

"I saw your mount. He passed right by me. That's why I came after you. Bears—and quite an assortment of other wildlife as well—are quite common in this area."

"You must think I'm a dunce."

"Well, you have a few things to learn about living in the bush. Where'd you come from, anyway?"

"Haiti. My parents were missionaries there."

"Were?"

She nodded. "Mama died a few months ago from a fever. Daddy got sick, too, and decided to retire. Uncle Sheldon— he was my father's brother—left us Misty Hills when he passed away a couple years ago, so we came here." Her voice held the semblance of a tremor, and she shivered again.

Dek slipped off his jacket and put it around her, holding it closed with one hand as he drew her back against himself.

Raine was surprised at his kindness, especially after the way he had acted the first few times their paths had crossed. She wondered how he could find the way home in the moonless night. Even through her sweatshirt she could feel the warmth still retained by his leather jacket. Snuggling into it, she relaxed slightly, and her hand moved to draw it tighter, inadvertently settling over his for an instant. She quickly removed hers.

But in that instant the feeling of it registered in her

brain. Extremely smooth, like satin, yet corded. Raine closed her eyes for a second with a shock of realization. Scars. Something had happened to him in his past that had left him scarred. Terribly. She swallowed.

Reaching the gate to Misty Hills, Dek drew Blackjack to a stop.

"I don't know how to thank you," Raine said. "I was never so frightened in my life."

"Just lucky I was nearby," he answered evenly, easing her down. Clancy nuzzled against her hand.

"I guess he's ready to be friends," Raine said, stroking a long silky ear.

"Try not to get caught like that again, huh?" Dek scolded gently. "Take a rifle with you."

She slipped off his coat and held it up, watching his dark silhouette as he put it on. "I'm afraid of guns," she said.

"So are bears." Thumbing the brim of his hat, he clucked his tongue and rode off, the dog right behind him.

Raine trudged toward the house. As she approached it, her father swung the door open wide and grabbed her in a fierce hug.

"Thank you, Lord," he said against her ear.

His embrace made breathing almost impossible. She wanted very much to cry, and just managed to retain control. "I'm so sorry, Daddy. I didn't mean to worry you."

"When the horse came back without you, I didn't know where in the world to start looking."

"Storm came home?"

"Of course." Easing his hold, he drew her inside and closed the door. "Horses know where they live, you know."

Raine shook her head in wonder. "Doesn't that beat all!" Then she burst into tears.

Riding the two miles down the dirt road to his cabin, Dek drew a deep breath, trying to banish the scent of Raine Montrose's perfumed hair from his nostrils. Annie's hair had smelled pretty like that. Forcing the sad reminder aside, he concentrated on his new neighbor. Missionary kid, he thought with disdain. Great. That's all he needed. Somebody preaching at him about the Almighty and His mercy. With a scowl he urged his horse across the creek to the corral.

Half an hour after she'd gotten home, Raine lowered herself into a tub of hot bubbles and scrunched down until they tickled her chin. She closed her eyes. Poor Daddy had been so concerned his face had taken on a few new lines. She'd have to be more careful. A leftover tremor coursed through her as she relived the fearful experience. She could have been left in that tree all night—and even in the morning might have taken hours to find her way. The bear could have come after her. She exhaled slowly, parting the foam with her breath. A rifle was out of the question. But maybe she could get a good big dog.

She smiled to herself at her reaction when Clancy had first charged her way a few days ago—and then again when he had pawed the tree beneath her tonight. She'd been so sure he was a wolf that she hadn't even been brave enough to look down at him. Thank heaven Dek happened by. Or was sent by.

The memory of Alan Decker's rich bass voice washed over her. Even if he had thought her a fool, to his credit he hadn't mentioned it. He'd been quite considerate of her feelings. Someone who truly disliked her would have been far less decent about the whole episode.

Raine could still feel the silken, translucent skin on his hand she'd accidentally touched. What could have happened to him that he'd been left so scarred?

four

Morning light spilled across Raine's bed as she stretched and yawned. She swung the covers aside and got up. Goodness, it was eight o'clock, already. She hadn't even heard her father stir, and he'd always been an early bird. Pulling on her aqua fleece robe, she slid her feet into matching slippers. Then she ran a brush through her hair and padded to the kitchen.

A refrigerator magnet pinned a note to the appliance door: "Hope I didn't wake you. Going to Red Deer with Jim Wilcox to look at cars. Back later. Dad. P.S. The horses are fed."

Raine smiled, then poured coffee and warmed it in the microwave, helping herself to a blueberry muffin from a plate on the counter.

After showering and dressing, she went to the big keyhole desk to one side of the fireplace and took out stationery and a pen, then started a letter:

> Hi Sarah,
>
> Sure was a treat to get your letter. Almost made me homesick—even though I promised myself I'd never give Haiti a single thought for the rest of my life! I had no idea how much I'd miss being with you.
>
> Dad and I have been pretty busy getting settled. We're quite happy to be in Canada again, though we pretend it doesn't matter that Mom isn't with us or that Mark decided to stay behind. The ranch is beautiful, and the area around us is so magnificent I find myself outside exploring a lot of the time, or else inside admiring it through the window. There's

so much to see.

> *Remember how I used to like to draw in school? Well I finally have time to do it to my heart's content. I found some sketching things in one of the drawers here and have been putting them to good use.*

> *You won't believe this, but I met someone really mysterious. One of our neighbors. I stumbled across his property accidentally, and he was very unfriendly. He seems to keep to himself, so I've never actually seen him up close.*

Sitting back against the chair, Raine rested an elbow on the desk and lifted her gaze, tapping the pen against her cheek. How much should she write, when she knew almost nothing about Alan Decker? She sighed, then continued.

> *I was sad to hear about our sweet little Dani. I do miss her a lot. Sometimes I find myself looking over my shoulder, expecting her to be tagging along. I'll probably never see her again. You'd better take good care of her for me, you hear?*

> *I hope you're able to come for a visit. We have tons of room in this big house—you'd even have one of your own. Keep after your father. He's bound to give in eventually!*

> *Guess I'll close for now. Write soon.*
> > *Love,*
> > *R.*

Raine took the letter out to the mailbox and raised the flag, then went back to the house. Not at all eager to repeat yesterday's scare, she did some laundry, then curled up by the fire with the novel she had started days ago.

By supper time her father had still not returned. She tended the horses for the night. The place had seemed lonely all day, but at least they would finally have a car. She gazed up at the empty road as she walked back to the house.

Reaching for the latch, Raine noticed that her tote bag lay on the stoop. She'd completely forgotten it when she'd seen the bear, her only thought being escape. But how—

Only one person could have found it and delivered it to her door. She shot a glance toward the main gate and the lane, but Alan Decker was not to be seen. She carried her things inside.

She emptied the contents on the table and found everything there. How thoughtful it had been of him, she thought, to have gone all the way back to that pond for her belongings. She only hoped he hadn't looked at her sketches. She had so much to learn, and the textbook on perspective hadn't been much help at all. Idly she flipped through the pages of her tablet.

Her cheeks flamed.

Not only had he *seen* them, he'd *corrected* them! Upon closer examination, she noted that the right third of each picture had been vastly improved. He'd written a comment: 'Never be afraid of the dark—especially in a drawing. Dek.' Her initial embarrassment subsided as she studied the sketches. He had only added shading, yet his portion had far greater depth than hers, adding the much needed dimension which had somehow eluded her.

A slow smile made its way over Raine's lips.

The next afternoon, a plate of fresh brownies in hand, she knocked on Alan Decker's door. She heard a low growl coming from inside, then a bark. The curtain in one of the windows flanking the door moved a fraction.

Several seconds passed.

Frowning, Raine knocked again.

Just as on their first encounter, the door opened an inch. Dek peered out through the narrow space.

"Hello," she said with a smile.

He didn't respond at first, merely perused her there on his doorstep.

Raine swallowed her confusion. "Sorry to bother you. I just wanted—Here." She held out the dish. "I baked these for you—to thank you for your assistance the other night, and for bringing my things by."

"It wasn't necessary to repay me," Dek said coolly. "I happened to be nearby."

"Well, all the same, you rescued me, and I wanted to thank you."

"And you have. Just leave the goodies on the porch chair, thanks." He gave a curt nod and closed the door.

Raine's mouth dropped open as she stood rooted in place. Leave the goodies on the chair? That would be the day. "Hey. You're not being fair, you know," she called out, her nose high in the air.

The knob turned, and the crack reappeared. "Fair?"

"Yes, fair. I came all the way down here to do the proper thing, and you—"

The edge of his mouth quirked. "You sure are persistent, I'll give you that. But you've thanked me, okay? Go home, Raine."

Dek watched her eyes narrow. They were the most unusual green color he'd ever seen, and they had the most direct way of looking right into his. Now sparking with anger as she stood there, they compelled him to 'be fair,' as she'd put it. Expelling a breath, he shook his head and lowered his gaze. "Sorry. I don't get a lot of company here."

Her expression eased. "I don't doubt it."

Despite himself, Dek laughed.

He had nice teeth, Raine decided, from what she could see of them, though one—his right eye tooth—slightly overlapped the one in front of it. But there was something definitely unnerving about the situation. "Do you have any idea how ridiculous it feels to be out here trying to talk, with you practically barricaded behind that slab of wood?" she asked.

"Oh, really?" It remained the same.

Raine closed her eyes for a second, then opened them again. "Look. Dek." She combed her fingers through her bangs. "I saw the changes you made in my sketches. I wanted to talk to you about them."

"What about them?"

"Come on. You made them better. I knew they lacked something, but I didn't know what it was. When I saw how you improved them, I realized it was the shading that I'd gotten wrong."

"It's a common mistake."

"Is it? How would you know that?" She shook her head. "Do you realize I don't know anything at all about you? What are you, an artist or something?"

"Sort of."

Raine grimaced. "I suppose that should account for the temperament," she said wryly.

He grinned.

"Well, to be honest, I do know one other thing."

"And what might that be?"

"I know you have some scars."

The smile vanished, and he glared. "Oh, so that's it. You're into the pity bit. Is that why you're really here?"

"No, it's not! Where on earth did you acquire such a

complex? A person's worth has absolutely nothing to do with his appearance."

Dek gave a bitter laugh. "Right."

"Look," Raine began. "Accidents are nothing new to me. I've been around them all my life, helping out at the medical clinic where my parents worked. I've seen severe injuries. I've seen horrible infections that led to loss of limbs. I've seen burns. I've even watched people die. From what I can tell, you're still healthy and strong. You're able to live a normal life from one day to the next—even if it is in hiding, feeling sorry for yourself." Alarmed at her own bluntness, she softened her voice. "And I sure could use a friend in this foreign country I'm living in."

Dek studied her. Why couldn't she just have stayed where she was—Haiti, hadn't she said? Why had she come to the haven he'd found, this sanctuary beyond people's self-conscious glances and embarrassed stares. All he wanted was to be left alone. And yet, here stood this guileless slip of a girl before him offering friendship . . . and perhaps even meaning it. Hopes and reservations conducted a minor skirmish inside as he considered whether or not she were serious. Then an element of resignation rose. If she *wasn't* serious, what better way to rid himself of her than by giving her what she'd come for. Scaring her off. It'd be quick, simple. End of problem.

Setting his jaw, he opened the door and took a step back, steeling himself for her repulsion, her horror.

"Well, here you are, lady," he said quietly. "Take a good look at the disfigured hulk who lives in the woods." He lifted his head and turned it to give her the full effect.

Raine's throat tightened as Dek's six-foot-two frame towered over her. For one brief heartbeat she did want to pity him as he stood before her vulnerable and exposed. He had the most striking face she had ever seen, with an olive complexion and incredible cheekbones. She let her gaze take in his dark, almost-black curly hair, the matching thick brows, eyes deep-set and light brown that even now peered at her down a straight Roman nose. She noted the pronounced five o'clock shadow which followed the contours of a strong chin, then abruptly stopped just left of it, where the natural pigmentation of his coloring ended. That third of his face bore waxy, fibrous, keloidal scars, a marbled mass of maroon, rose, and sallow pink all the way to his misshapen ear and continuing downward on his neck. The collar of his shirt concealed any further damage from view.

She met his stare. "I've seen worse."

Dek leveled his astonished gaze. She hadn't so much as caught her breath or flinched. In fact, she hadn't even blinked.

"Now here," she said, handing him the brownies. "These are for you."

He took them. Clancy rose with casual interest from beside an oxblood leather recliner. He came and sat beside Dek's feet.

Raine smiled and looked again at Dek. "I do have to go now, but would it be okay to come by again for some help with my art? I really would like to learn how to do it right. If you have the time, of course."

"It's up to you." There, he told himself. She still had an escape. Raine Montrose would never darken his door again.

Letting herself out, Raine forced herself to walk at a normal pace to where she had tied Storm. Reaching him, she turned with a smile and waved, hoping against hope that Alan Decker couldn't see the tears that had spilled over her lashes before she'd reached the bottom porch step and even now made rosy splotches on her pink blouse.

Several groups of people milled about the Community Baptist Church on the southwest corner of town as Raine and her father arrived that Sunday morning.

A wiry, sandy-haired man of medium build, who appeared to be in his late twenties, stepped away from the door of the white, aluminum-sided building and hurried down the steps toward the parking lot. He waited as they pulled into an available space, then strolled toward them while they exited the cream-colored Chevrolet sedan. He raised a hand in greeting. "Welcome. We're glad to see you folks this morning. I'm Steve Grogan, the pastor here."

Raine smiled, noting his friendly manner and twinkling light blue eyes. Straight gold eyebrows the same shade as his hair reminded her of her brother's, and for an instant she felt a stab of homesickness for Mark.

"How do you do," her father said, closing the car door. He extended his hand, which the young man clasped warmly. "Lucas Montrose. This," he indicated with his head, "is my daughter, Lorraine."

Pastor Grogan nodded her way, and in the flicker of a second, shot an appreciative glance over her as he reached to shake her hand. "Nice to meet you both." His strong grip lingered but a moment. He gestured toward the front door. "Come right on in. I'll start you off with a few introductions."

Raine took a steadying breath and preceded the men up the steps and into the church, where the minister rattled off names of individuals who stood and smiled politely and seemed genuinely friendly as she and her father passed each dark walnut pew. She knew she'd be weeks sorting out which name belonged to which person, and felt relief at the first familiar face.

Molly Griffith and her husband, Glenn, a barrel-chested

man with the massive arms of a lumberjack and a pronounced underbite, were seated in a row mid-way up the aisle. "Well, how nice to be seein' you an' your father out this mornin'," Molly beamed, giving a nudge to her mate. "See, didn't I tell you she was a pretty little bit of a thing?"

Raine blushed and dropped her gaze.

"Sure did. You're right." The man grinned and shook her father's hand. "Glad to have you both here."

"Nice to meet you folks," came her father's voice.

The first notes sounded from the church organ.

"Well, that's my cue," the pastor said. "We'd better finish this after the service. With a good-natured wave, he strode up to the platform and sat on one of three burgundy upholstered chairs, while Raine and her father chose the row behind the Griffiths.

Raine scanned the sanctuary. Color fragments from the arched, stained glass windows reflected upon eggshell walls, and a succession of walnut studs met in the arched ceiling. A back-lit wooden cross hung on the wall behind the pulpit.

The song leader, a tall, loose-jointed man with receding auburn hair, opened in prayer, then led two lively hymns.

When it came time for the sermon, Pastor Grogan stepped to the pulpit, looking calm and confident in an immaculate, double-breasted pinstripe suit; "In our continuing series on well-known Psalms, this morning we're going to study the all-time favorite, the Twenty-third Psalm." He opened the Bible he'd brought to the pulpit, then scanned the worshipers.

Raine wondered if she imagined that his gaze lingered on her. She transferred her attention to locating the reference in her Bible, then opened her purse and took out the small notebook she used for taking sermon notes. Following along as the pastor read the passage, she found herself comparing his pleasant yet average voice to Alan Decker's rich, deep modulations. Moistening her lips, she shot a nonchalant glance around the congregation to see if Dek might have come, then called herself a fool for the hundredth time.

"... And I shall dwell in the house of the Lord forever," the minister said, finishing the last verse. "A good many messages one might hear on this psalm of David are centered on its reference to the Lord as the shepherd of a vast flock of needy sheep who follow Him. And rightly so. There's comfort in the knowledge that we are in His care at all times and that He is concerned about what happens to us.

"But as I studied in preparation for today's sermon, I felt led to center our thoughts on the fourth verse, where it speaks of the valley of the shadow of death. All of us live in that dark shadow, knowing that at any time we may be called Home. But often the real pain of it comes not from our own death, but actually from the loss of someone dear. Before we begin, let us pray."

Raine tapped a finger apprehensively on the silver-edged pages of her open Bible and closed her eyes. She didn't want to think about death, not since it had shattered her world. During the prayer she found herself wishing she and her father had chosen next Sunday for their first visit here.

"Amen," Pastor Grogan said, then raised his head, a composed expression on his face as he gathered his thoughts. "The Angel of Death," he said finally, "is never a welcome visitor. Those who belong to God can face death without fear, however, and even with peace, for the end of the trials of life here on earth marks the joyous beginning of eternity in Heaven. We read in First Corinthians that Jesus defeated death at His resurrection, thereby taking away its sting. But we'll leave that for another message and concentrate instead, this morning, upon those whom death leaves behind. The ones who have walked into the valley and felt the empty, cold shadow."

Raine felt the breath leave her body with the remembrance of the dark emptiness which had dampened her existence a mere eight months ago when her mother had succumbed to influenza. Trembling, she closed her Bible and forcefully blocked out the minister's voice by composing a letter to Sarah in her mind. In it she went into great detail over all the minute aspects of every single day that had passed since the last time she had written, only barely conscious of the voice droning on in the background. Just when she decided to get up and spend the remainder of the service in the rest room, she noticed a sudden quiet.

Pastor Grogan smiled at the congregation. "Before we dismiss with prayer, I'd like to invite everyone present to stay for the potluck. I'm sure the ladies have outdone last month's feast. We can take this opportunity to make Lucas Montrose and his daughter, Lorraine, feel welcome. Now let's close in prayer."

In the mint green basement of the church, long tables covered by plain white roll paper sat end to end, providing ample space for the people who'd attended the service. Molly and Glenn Griffith steered Raine and her father to a prominent spot near the front, and they all took adjoining seats along one side.

Delicious aromas wafted from the kitchen. Ladies scurried about completing last-minute reheating and setting heaped bowls and platters onto the double serving table on the kitchen end of the open room.

"I feel embarrassed that we didn't bring anything," Raine admitted to Molly.

"Nonsense." the older lady replied, fussing with a pleat on the bodice of her plaid dress. She looked up, her round eyes twinkling. "Who ever heard of a food shortage at a potluck?"

"Hope we can eat pretty soon. My stomach is about to growl," Mr. Griffith added. "Come on, Lucas," he said getting up. "You should meet Harry Van Dyke." The two left for the other end of the room, where a handful of men congregated in a mildly boisterous cluster.

"Well," Molly said. "Much as I hate abandoning you, I'd better take my salad out of the fridge and see if they need help out there. Back in a jiffy." She hurried away.

Raine smiled after her and sighed. She set her purse on the floor beside her feet, then laced her fingers together as she tried not to feel out of place among the new faces. She still felt unease leftover from the subject of the morning message, but lifted her chin and concentrated on her surroundings.

"Deserted already, I see."

She looked up into Pastor Grogan's smiling face. "So it appears."

"Well, not for long." He motioned to the slender brunette who had played the organ during the service, and the young lady excused herself from a pair of white-haired women and made her way over.

"Francie," the pastor said upon her approach. "We need a bit of your warm charm here. This is Lorraine Montrose. Lorraine," he said, transferring his gaze to her, "I'd like you to meet Frances Shipley, our organist."

"How do you do, Lorraine," Frances said. Her smile revealed perfect teeth.

Fitting, Raine thought, looking at the rest of her. Huge long-lashed turquoise eyes, porcelain skin, and an expressive mouth—not to mention an abundant long mane of rich chestnut hair. "Very nice to meet you."

"Well, I'll leave you two to get acquainted," the preacher said, moving away.

"We're always glad to see new people in the service," Frances said politely. Ringless tapered fingers combed the deep wave which fell across her forehead from a side part.

Raine smiled and nodded, watching the girl's eyes follow the pastor as he strode with easy strides to a group of teenagers and clamped a hand on the shoulder of one of the boys. She looked back at Frances. "I enjoyed your playing this morning. Especially 'Blessed Quietness' during the offering. It's one of my favorites."

"Thank you. It was a request."

Her polite yet shy and reserved manner made Raine miss Sarah all the more and intensified the wish that her friend would be able to come for a visit.

"Will you be coming to worship regularly?" Frances asked, removing a loose thread from her blue-green, silky dress.

"Most likely. My father seems to be making friends."

"How nice. Then we'll probably be seeing each other quite a lot. Perhaps we can have lunch together sometime."

"I'd like that."

The sound of a spoon being tapped against a glass interrupted their conversation. The room grew quiet and the minister raised a hand. "Everything's ready. so we'll ask the blessing on all this wonderful food we've been smelling."

On the drive home afterward, Daddy's voice cut across Raine's thoughts. "My, but those folks are friendly."

"Seems like."

"And that pastor, Steve. Great fellow. I invited him to come for supper one day next week."

"What?"

"He's not married, you know. Said he'd like to come out and get to know us, since we'll be joining the church."

Raine's fingers curled into her palms. She wasn't quite ready to start socializing with people she didn't know, especially unattached males. But there was no mistaking that gleam in her father's eye.

five

Raine set the platter in the center of the tablecloth and removed the half-apron protecting her jade linen dress, then gave a quick once over to make sure everything was in place. Satisfied, she smiled to her father through the sitting room archway. "It's ready."

"Good," he said, clapping his palms onto his knees and getting up. "We've been summoned, Steve."

"Everything certainly smells delicious," the minister said. He rose, allowing his host to precede him.

At her chair, Raine gestured for the young man to take the seat across from her as her father sat in his customary place at the head. She fought the ridiculous nervousness she felt around the pastor. Steven Grogan was their guest, and despite her uneasiness about having him spend an evening here, she would be a gracious hostess. It was only one night. He did look rather attractive in his brown tweed sportcoat and café-au-lait slacks, she thought grudgingly, then chided herself. Of course she'd have noticed his appearance. Artists were naturally observant.

"Would you do the honors?" her father asked, turning to Steve.

"Glad to." He bowed his head.

Catching herself watching the glow from the oak and hobnail chandelier dance over his sandy hair, Raine quickly closed her eyes. In this light he looked even more like her brother.

"Most gracious heavenly Father, we do thank You for the kind hospitality of this home and the wonderful feast before

54

us. We ask Your blessing upon it and ask, too, that You keep Your hand upon us as we get to know each other. In Jesus name, amen."

"Amen," she whispered. Moistening her lips, she took a sip from her water goblet.

Her father picked up the platter and passed it to Steve. "Help yourself. Raine is a wonderful cook. You never have to be shy around here."

"Thanks. You don't have to ask me twice." Forking a generous slice of roast pork onto his plate, he passed it to Raine. "The best meals I have are at the homes of my members. I'm not so hot in the kitchen, myself."

Typical helpless male, Raine decided, then scolded herself for being uncharitable.

"Eat out a lot, do you?" her father asked.

"Not really. The church families take pity on the poor bachelor, so they take turns coddling me. Not that I mind, you understand. I appreciate their kindness."

No doubt, Raine thought sarcastically. What's worse than having to eat one's own cooking? Her family might have enjoyed the luxury of eating somewhere other than home once in awhile, too, but on the mission field they were glad just to have time to eat at all. Giving herself a mental shake, she looked at Steven just as he shifted his gaze her way.

His eyes looked a clear blue in contrast to his cream shirt. He ate a chunk of meat and swallowed. "I must say this is delicious."

"Thank you." She managed not to blush.

"Takes after her mama," her father said. "Real good in the kitchen." He stabbed carrot rounds, stacking several on the tines of his fork. "So where did you graduate from school? Hope you don't mind my curiosity."

Steve swallowed and shot him a grin. "Not at all. Prairie Bible Institute, in Three Hills. Then I went on to Denver Theological and took further graduate studies in Toronto. I've been here for two years now."

"Well, that's quite an impressive list. But all those years, and you never came across one nice Christian girl you wanted to marry?"

Raine almost choked at her father's question, but recovered as the pastor laughed.

"Well, I wouldn't say that, exactly. More like too many!" He paused, and his grin faded. "Actually, there was someone I had my eye on, back home in Saskatchewan. She was supposed to wait for me to finish my training. But unfortunately ...." His eyes made a self-conscious switch to his plate.

After a short silence, Raine cleared her throat and rose. "I think the coffee's finished. I'll get it." The few minutes away from her father's maneuvers came as a relief. She filled the cream pitcher and put it on a tray beside the sugar bowl and coffee pot. Returning to the dining room, she heard her father change the topic.

"Still have some family back there in Saskatchewan, Steve?"

"Yes sir, I do. My parents run a farm implement business, and I have three younger sisters. But say, enough about me. I came out here to get to know you folks."

After setting the tray on the table, Raine filled their cups and took her seat.

Steven added cream and two spoons of sugar to his brew and stirred determinedly, his spoon clinking against the china for what seemed a whole minute. "So, how did you enjoy the work in Haiti?" he asked, turning to his host. "A hospital, you said, right? You're a doctor?"

"No, an electrical engineer. But I can fix just about anything that needs it, which is a real asset for a missionary. My wife was a nurse, though, and our son did go on to medical school. He stayed on at the clinic after we left. He's only recently married one of the new arrivals on the field, and tells me I'm to be a grandfather next spring."

"Well," Steve said, nodding with sincere interest. "That's certainly something to look forward to." He turned his attention to Raine. "And what about you, Lorraine? Are you a nurse, too?"

She blotted her mouth on her napkin. "No, not really. I did have some of the training, but I was just an aide."

"Just an aide!" her father said. "Listen to that. She was a great help in the summers while on hiatus from the boarding schools in Mexico and Florida. After she graduated we appreciated having her full time. She often filled in over at the office and offered a helping hand wherever else she was needed."

"I don't doubt it," Steve said, then turned toward Raine again. "Do you miss it?"

Miss it? Raine thought. The never ending line of sick, hurting people? The days that never seemed to have enough hours? As far as she was concerned, if she never helped another living soul for the rest of her life that would be fine. Then a little girl's dark face came to mind, one with huge black eyes, frail limbs, and a smile that could melt a heart. "Sometimes I miss the people."

"Yes, gentle folk they are, for the most part," Dad said. "Always such a great need there."

"I couldn't agree more," Steven replied. "You must have had some incredible experiences over the years. I'm sure the congregation would appreciate it if some Sunday evening you could relate some of those stories in church. People often get so wrapped up in their own lives, they forget there are still those on this earth who've never met a Christian or heard the Gospel. It's good to put out reminders from time to time that the Lord's servants still need support and prayers."

"I'd enjoy that," her father answered.

The pastor looked again in Raine's direction. "And what kind of plans might you have for the future, Lorraine, now that you've left the mission? Will you be looking for a job of some kind?"

"Not just yet. I'm sort of taking a vacation and concentrating on my art, now that I have some time."

"Hm." He thought for a moment. "How about considering something in the meantime? The ladies missionary society would probably enjoy having you bring the devotional some month. What do you say?"

She shook her head. "No, please. I'm not much of a speaker."

"Nonsense. Sweet ladies like Molly Griffith and old Bertha Sinclair would really like hearing what it was like growing up as a missionary kid, I'm sure. How you watched the hand of the Lord at work around you, that sort of thing. It wouldn't by any means have to be anything structured or formal."

"All the same," she said, meeting his stare, "I'd prefer not to."

Steve relaxed against his chair with a good-natured smile. "Well, I'm not known for giving up easily."

"And she's not known for giving in," her father teased.

"Daddy!"

The skin beside his eyes crinkled with mischief as he exchanged conspiratorial glances with the minister. "Sorry. Couldn't resist that one. It might be fun, you know, talking about what it was like living in some other part of the world. I find ladies groups especially easy to talk to."

Raine envisioned herself walking calmly up to some podium and meeting the eyes of a roomful of strangers . . . then forgetting every word she'd planned to say. There couldn't be a worse way to spend some 'enjoyable' night. "I . . . I don't think so."

"Well," the minister said. "There's a time for everything, and all that. I'm not going to pressure you. Yet." A flash of strong white teeth accompanied his grin.

"Then neither will I," her father added. "You might feel more comfortable around the ladies once you get to know them." He cleared his throat. "I sure could use some of that splendid blueberry cream cake you made, though . . ."

After dessert, Lucas led the way back to the sitting room couch and got out some slides from Haiti, along with a hand viewer. "You might enjoy some of these," he told Steven.

"Yes, I would."

"This first group shows our facilities there and some of the staff. This one is my son, Mark, and his wife, Ruth."

Taking the viewer, Steven examined the first shot.

Over the young man's head, Lucas watched Raine as she cleared the table. She looked real pretty in her green dress. He had hoped she'd be relaxed and open around their guest. But though she'd been extremely polite, she'd also been reserved and unaccountably remote. He himself felt drawn to the minister, and could envision including him at a lot of future get-togethers. Eventually Raine would come around. After all, she was of age. The time had come for her to start considering something in her future besides art, and she could do a lot worse than to take up with a fine young man like Steven Grogan. He'd have to encourage her along that line

Winter put a definite period on the golden sentence written by Indian summer some weeks ago, and obliterated even the memory of October's last colorful days with a blanket of snow. Enthralled, Raine watched great feathery flakes dance and swirl on the wind, then finally land on the earth and pile up before her eyes.

Her father walked up behind her at the dining room window and put an arm around her shoulders.

"It has to be the prettiest sight I've ever seen," she murmured. "Even better than calendar pictures."

"Yes." He gave a squeeze. "Winter was my favorite time as I grew up. I missed it once we moved south."

Raine slid him a sideways glance. "You liked being cold, Daddy?"

"Well, no, not that. It's other things I remember, like how Shel and I would run to the radio first thing after a blizzard, praying that the schools would close so we could stay home."

"And did they?"

"Sometimes. We'd bundle up and head outside to build snow forts. We had the greatest snowball fights, Sheldon, me, and the other boys from around our place. By the time we went in, we'd be half frozen, and Ma would have hot chocolate ready, with lots of marshmallows."

"Sounds like fun."

"Yes. Those were the days." He inhaled slowly and expelled a deep breath. "Many times Pa's old car would get stuck in a bank of snow, and we'd have to get the horses to pull it out. But best of all I liked the good sleigh Pa always kept. That thing could get around fine when the car couldn't. He'd let us drive it all over the place. I even took your mom for a few rides back in the beginning to impress her with my skill and finesse."

With a smile, Raine hugged him. "Must have been like one of those old black and white films I saw once in awhile at boarding school. With everyone dressed in thick coats, huddling under a wool blanket, and the harness bells jingling with each hoofbeat."

"That's how it was, all right." He nodded slowly, as if lost in the old times. "Wonder if Shel's old sleigh might still be out in one of the sheds."

The phone rang just then, and he strode to answer it. "Hello?" He paused. "Sure, she's right here. Hold on."

Surprised, Raine crossed the room and took the receiver. "Hello?"

"Hi, Lorraine. Steve. I was wondering if I might interest you in a play tomorrow evening."

"A play?" she asked inanely.

"Yes. The high school play is coming up. They're doing 'Fiddler on the Roof.' Are you familiar with the story?"

"No, not really."

"All the better. It's about a Jewish family just before the Bolshevik revolution in Russia. Quite a touching storyline. I think you'd enjoy it."

Raine thought it sounded intriguing. "Well, okay. Sure. I'd be glad to."

"Great. I'll pick you up at six, then. We'll grab a bite to eat in town and go see the play."

"All right. See you tomorrow." As she hung up, she met her father's more than pleased expression.

"Steve's taking you out, huh? Splendid." Turning on his heel, he went and stoked the fire.

Raine watched him for a moment, taking note of the broad smile puffing out his cheeks. She'd accepted a date with the minister, but that didn't necessarily mean anything serious would develop—if that was what her father was contemplating. After all, the last thing she needed right now was to try to hold her own in deep theological discussions. It was stretching her to the limit just to read a simple chapter in Proverbs or a Psalm. She'd be way out of her depth with a preacher. "I think I'll go for a walk."

Outside, she gave her scarf an extra wrap around her neck, amazed at how much colder today was than yesterday. She tucked the wrists of her mittens securely inside her sleeve cuffs and shoved her hands into the pockets of her down jacket. Snow muffled the usual outdoor noises, lending a hush to the world. Now the loudest sound heard was the shush of wind over the new drifts. She lifted her face toward the white sky and watched amazed as millions of snowflakes filled her vision, dark specks of moisture against the bright clouds. She caught a few on her tongue, and they melted instantly. She felt ten years old.

Her boots made deep impressions as she strolled past the outbuildings and made a wide circuit of the ranch, awed by the vista surrounding her in whites and grays. Late afternoon light brought a slight lavender hue to the shadows, breaking up the basic monochromatic scheme. Coming to one of the stonewalls which framed the edges of the property, Raine brushed some snow off the top and leaned back against it, elbows resting on the rocks as she drank in the scene. Not too much farther away was Dek's place. Was it too soon to call on him again?

A sound to her left caught her interest, and she shifted her attention toward it, seeing a small tractor with a plow attached coming up the lane. She watched it draw closer. Then she saw a familiar figure at the wheel, and turned with a smile.

Dek lifted a gloved hand in greeting as he made one pass

up the right side of the lane. Running parallel with him in the opposite ditch, O'Clancy bounded through snow higher than the tops of his fur-covered legs.

At the main road, the plow made a U-turn and came back, stopping beside the stonewall where Raine waited. "What do you think of winter?" he called over the noise of the engine, then shut it off as the dog ran playfully ahead.

Raine smiled, taking note of the thick scarf he wore tied under his black hat, shielding his scars from the elements. "I've never seen anything like it. Will it be like this till spring?"

His nose glowed from the chill as he returned her smile with a lopsided one of his own. "No, it comes and goes. Some years we hardly get any snow at all, then other times it starts in September and keeps snowing off and on till June. But even then we have chinooks to warm us up."

"Chinooks?" Her breath came out on a misty cloud.

"Masses of warm air from the Pacific," Dek said, studying her, noticing the fine white angora hairs on her hat and scarf playing against her face on the wind. "They break up the long winter for us. You'll see them coming, off to the west there."

He watched Raine look in the direction he indicated, then back to him.

"First thing you see," he continued, "is an arc of clouds on the horizon. The breeze that carries them along is warm, balmy. The temperature starts to shoot up . . . can be as much as forty degrees or so warmer within the hour."

"That can't be possible."

"Sure it is. Ask anybody."

"I will."

Dek smiled inwardly at Raine's look of challenge and tried

to convince himself he hadn't plowed the whole lane for the express purpose of catching a glimpse of her. It had been more than a week since she'd been by, but then he hadn't really expected her to come back. There was no reason for her to seek him out for companionship, not when she could walk around in the real world like everybody else. He'd just gotten used to seeing her all over the place and, like a fool, had somehow begun to enjoy it. It was ridiculous.

He clutched the gear shift tighter. Why was he even having these stupid thoughts? He'd been a miserable failure with Annie, hadn't been able to protect her when she'd most needed it. He didn't deserve a relationship with anyone else, much less some girl who was easily a good ten years younger than himself and had led an extremely sheltered life besides. More than likely she'd come up with a whole raft of more convenient pursuits these days, just like he figured she would, for all her alleged interest in developing her art.

"It must be fun to sketch snow scenes," she said.

"Huh?" *Had she read his mind?* he wondered.

"Or even paint them," she went on. "Do you paint?"

"I used to."

"I thought I'd seen some framed oils in your house when I was there. Yours?"

He nodded.

"I'll have to look closer next time."

She couldn't have said that. He was sure. But those big emerald eyes transpierced his as she continued talking. He couldn't let them get to him.

"I'd really love to learn how to use oils or water colors. But I suppose they're way beyond me. It'll take forever to conquer the sketching first."

"Actually, you don't need to know everything about

drawing in order to paint," he said.

Again came her look of disbelief.

"Really. It's all illusion anyway. Easier than sketching."

She looked away, as if giving him a chance to correct the statement, then raised her long lashes his way. "Would you teach me sometime?"

A niggling suspicion began to make itself known: that starting anything up with Raine Montrose would be a very grave mistake. Nevertheless, he heard his own voice setting himself up for it. "Like I said before, it's up to you. The, uh, brownies were good, by the way."

She smiled warmly. "I'm glad you liked them. I'll bring you some more. Is there a particular day next week I might have a lesson?" Her smile made her eyes dance.

Dek coughed and looked away. He had struggled hard to find consolation in solitude. Perhaps it would be a mistake to forfeit all the ground he'd made. He should have stayed home. Inside, where the cold didn't make his scars burn.

She tipped her head when he failed to respond. "Oh, I'm sorry. You're probably busy."

"No," he blurted. "Not at all." What a jerk he was, he told himself. She only wanted a friend, someone who could give lessons in art. She didn't need anything beyond that. Neither did he. He forced a casual note into his voice. "I mean, whenever you have time is fine with me. Have you been working on any new drawings?"

She felt her cheeks pinken. "A few. I'm . . . sort of afraid to show them to you."

"Don't be silly. I won't bite your head off. Bring them with you. We have to start somewhere."

"They're probably not very good," she hedged.

"Why don't you let me be the judge of that?"

Raine let her gaze wander over his face. His expression puzzled her. Everything about him puzzled her. With a smile, she rubbed her hands together and hugged herself. "It's getting cold. I'd better get home."

"And I'd better plow the rest of the lane," he said. "See you."

Raine nodded and waved, walking backward as he started the motor and chugged away. Turning, she hurried toward the house. She had a lot of work to do on those new sketches before she let Dek see them.

Dek called himself all kinds of names under his breath as he rode home. The whole thing was unbelievable. He should have left well enough alone. Why did he have to go and complicate things by nosing up the lane? She had her own life. He had his. Even if it was one with only O'Clancy for company, at least he had been comfortable with it. There had been no one to answer to. What was he getting himself into?

six

Raine couldn't decide if it was relief she felt or apprehension at the sight of Steven Grogan's emerald Buick pulling into the drive. Her father had been grinning his ears off most of the day, and she'd sought consolation in her room a good part of the time as she worked on her new sketches. Now suddenly it was over. Steve was here. As her father let him in, she slipped on her high leather boots.

The kitchen door opened.

"Look who we have here," Dad said, giving Steve a mild shove in her direction.

Raine smiled thinly and reached for her indigo and violet plaid coat, draped over a chair back.

"Here, I'll get that for you," Steve said, holding it while she slid her arms into the sleeves.

"Thank you."

"Well," her father said. "You two have yourselves a real nice time."

Raine shot him a warning glare, and he winked.

"We'll do our best," the younger man answered, opening the door for her.

As they drove to town in the fading light, Raine watched the snowy landscape pass in a blur.

"Hope you like Italian food," Steve said, cutting into her musings.

"I like just about everything."

"Good. There's a new place called Mrs. D.'s that's only been open about a month or so. Excellent homemade fettuccine and ravioli. And the bread is out of this world."

"Sounds wonderful."

Raine couldn't help admiring the charming restaurant after their arrival, and from their quiet corner table she scanned the dark wooden furnishings, red and white checked linens, and candles glowing from red glass holders in the middle of each table. Lush plants hung at attractive intervals, their wrought iron brackets matching the design of the chandeliers.

After they had eaten, Steven checked his watch. "We're cutting it a bit close. We'd better head on over to the high school." Getting up, he left money on the table for the check, and they hurried out to his car.

They found a good percentage of the seats in the school auditorium filled when they got there. Steven led the way to the refreshment table, where they got styrofoam cups of coffee. After lacing his liberally with sugar, he guided Raine to two vacant chairs on the outside end of the third row.

"Can you see okay?" he asked after they'd sat down.

"Yes, fine. I'm surprised there's such a crowd."

"Well, the students do quite a good job with the productions, so they always have a fair turnout. A few cast members are young people from our church, by the way. I'll point them out." He settled back and relaxed.

The recorded prelude stopped, and a teenage girl in peasant costume came from backstage to a microphone on one end of the platform. She smiled and waited until the applause died down. "Ladies and gentlemen, welcome to this evening's performance, 'Fiddler on the Roof.' We hope you enjoy it."

The rousing theme song began, and Raine found herself looking forward to the play which followed. She felt drawn at once into the storyline and hated to see the final curtain as she self-consciously dabbed her eyes.

On the way home afterward, Raine winced with chagrin. "Sorry I fell apart in that last scene," she said. "It was so touching. They did a terrific portrayal of the time period and the hardships that come with change."

"Yes, they did. It's tough to go against one's heritage—especially when it comes to faith, however misplaced it might be. Imagine waiting all these hundreds and hundreds of years for a Messiah who's already come and gone. That's the real sorrow."

Raine pondered the thought.

"Well, anyway," he said, guiding the car through the gate of Misty Hills and stopping at the house, "I'm glad you came this evening."

"I enjoyed it, too. Would you like to come inside? I'm sure Daddy has coffee ready and waiting."

"Better not. I have a long day tomorrow. One of our members is scheduled for surgery in Calgary. I'll walk you to the door, though." Getting out, he crossed to her side and lent her a hand.

"Well, thank you for inviting me, Steven. I had a really nice time."

"Good. Might I ask you again sometime?"

She shrugged. "My treat?"

"Well, I don't know about that," he said with a grin. "I'm not quite that modern in my thinking. We'll see, huh? 'Night."

"Goodnight."

Inside, to her surprise, Raine found everything still and only one lamp glowing in the sitting room. She clicked it off on her way to her room.

As she undressed, her thoughts kept returning to the evening performance: to the funny lines that even yet made her smile and to the sad ones that had her struggling to keep tears inside. She'd been especially glad Steven had been a

gentleman. Even that brought thoughts of Mark, who had the
same way of holding his head and many similar mannerisms.
The pastor's comment about misplaced faith still bothered
her as she pulled on a brushed nylon nightgown and got
into bed. Did it really matter what a person believed, as
long as his heart was sincere? At one time she would have
agreed wholeheartedly. But since her mother's death, she
had been plagued by doubt.

Silence settled around her as her eyes adjusted to the
dark. The yard light outside glowed through her curtains,
softening the shapes of her furniture. It seemed especially
bright now as it reflected off the snow.

Snow. Snow scenes. On the last fringe of consciousness, she saw Dek on the tractor, smiling at her with those
sad brown eyes.

"And this," Raine's father said to the Sunday evening
congregation as he clicked the projector control to the next
slide, "is the clinic where we ministered to the Haitians. It was
constructed partly with native labor, paid for with private
funds before it ever opened its doors. Our modest facility
operates on the outskirts of Port-au-Prince, in an area where
conditions are especially ripe for disease. The founder of the
clinic, once a man of wealth and position in Britain, followed
the Lord's suggestion to a rich young ruler in the New
Testament and sold his possessions, deciding instead to go
where people were in need and serve the Lord there. This
very dear friend, Charles Claymore Hamilton—seen here
in this shot with his wife, Catherine, and daughter, Sarah—is now being blessed by God in ways beyond the
material. One day I'm sure he will be surprised at the
eternal reward that is waiting for him."

Raine watched the familiar photo, amazed at the feelings of homesickness that accompanied the sight of her best friend and the clinic. She had made a concentrated effort to forget how desperately the poor Haitian people needed someone who cared about them. But now that she thought back, it really hadn't been all that bad living there. She could have stayed on indefinitely, if it hadn't cost her mother's life. She immediately cut that thought off as another shot appeared on the screen.

"This," her dad continued, "is my son, Mark. He's a doctor now and recently married a medical assistant from our staff." He clicked to the next picture. "This is Mark with his wife, Ruth, and some of the other workers."

On the edge of the group shot, Raine saw Sarah again and felt every mile that now separated them. She decided that when she got home she'd write once more and beg Sarah to come. Several familiar pictures of the interior of the facility followed, increasing Raine's loneliness. She rose quietly and went to the restroom, lingering purposely to ensure that she wouldn't inadvertently see any slides of her mother. Shortly after she returned to her seat the room lights came on.

Steve crossed the platform and shook her father's hand. "I'm sure everyone appreciates your fine presentation this evening, Lucas. We hope this will be the first of many."

Her father nodded. "Anytime you say the word, I'll share the need." He stepped down and sat on the first pew.

"Before we close in prayer," the pastor continued, "I want to remind everyone about the offering plate on the back table. We'll forward this evening's love gifts to Dr. Mark Montrose for the needs of the mission in Haiti. Now let's bow our heads."

On the drive home, Lucas watched Raine out of the corner

of his eye. Chin drooping, she had barely spoken since church got out and even now toyed absently with one of the buttons on her coat. "You're quiet tonight."

"Am I?"

"Something on your mind?"

She shrugged, and when she blinked, a tear fell.

The sight brought a twinge to his own heart. "Sometimes it helps to talk."

Raine sighed and wiped her face with her fingers, then took a tissue from her pocket.

"Some things in life are beyond words," he said thoughtfully. "It was the slides, I'd imagine. Too many old memories, am I right?"

She met his eyes, then averted her own. "Oh, Daddy. Those pictures of the hospital, and everyone made me . . . lonesome . . . for Mama. I miss her so much." The last half came out on a sob, and in the glow of the dash lights, Lucas saw tears glistening on her cheeks.

He felt profound compassion. "I know, honey. Me, too. But she's still with us, you know. In our hearts."

Raine grimaced. "Sure. But is that enough for you?" Angrily, she swiped her nose with the tissue, but her words grew softer. "It isn't for me."

"What are you saying?"

"You know very well what I mean. Mom shouldn't have died. It wasn't fair of God to take her."

Lucas steered to the shoulder of the road and stopped. He turned off the ignition and turned to her. "Not fair of God?" he said in a gentle challenge. "How can you say such a thing—or even think it?"

"You want to know how? I'll tell you." Her voice sounded stronger now, and he knew it was reinforced by the strength of things she had kept inside for months. She went on. "Mama was perfectly fine until that last flu came around. You know that. She worked day and night helping other sick people, never even slowing down or resting herself. God shouldn't have taken her away from us, away from them. Why would He do something like that, anyway . . . let a person go to the mission field and then let her die? If He is so anxious for the Gospel to be spread around the world, to have people serving Him, why would He take away somebody who was out doing it? It's so senseless."

"Raine," he said. "I know you loved your mother a great deal. You were always very close to her, and you must miss her terribly. So do I, you know. She was part of my life—the very best part—for many, many years." He reached to brush a lock of hair from her eyes, but she shrank away. Breathing a quick prayer for wisdom, he tried to organize his thoughts in the heavy silence broken only by her occasional sniff, then began again.

"Sometimes when a person dies, it may seem like an accident to us, and something we could have stopped if only we'd tried hard enough. But you know, to the Lord it isn't like that at all. Everything happens in its own time, its own season."

"Oh, that's right. I forgot the passage somebody put in the Bible to make it easier to rationalize everything that happens to us," she rasped bitterly.

Lucas hid his shock. "It wasn't 'somebody' trying to excuse life's experiences, Raine. It was written by King Solomon, the wisest man who ever lived."

She stared at her hands without speaking.

"It also says in Psalms," he continued, "that at the moment we're conceived the Lord knows our names, and all our days are recorded in His book. *All our days,* did you hear that? And Job also wrote that our days are numbered. That doesn't mean we only have a few left, as some people might interpret it—though that could be true, too, in a way. But even more, it means they are numbered altogether, from the beginning to the end. God knows before we are born exactly how long our time on earth will be."

Blotting her nose again, Raine pursed her lips.

"The Bible says that God takes no pleasure in the death of the wicked, but the death of those who are His is precious in His sight. He delights in their arrival. He's been waiting for them—for us—to come Home, each of us at the appointed time, so He can bestow rewards for all that we've done for Him."

Raine listened without comment as he spoke. They were things she'd never particularly thought about before, and she clung to them like a drowning person would to a life preserver, letting the ideas soothe her.

"So you see," he went on, "it might have been before *our* time for your mama to go Home. It's hard for us to be without her. She was part of us, and we loved having her with us. . . . But it wasn't before God's time. None of us is guaranteed any amount of years, Raine. Our loved ones, our family, our friends, all our children—they're really only on loan for however many days are in the plan of God. All we can do is love them while we have them and not waste a day, because every day is precious. And it isn't given to us to know when a life may end."

Raine scrunched up the tissue, turning it round and round in her fist, wishing she had her father's deep convictions and knew the same peace. But her faith had drifted since her mother's death, and she sometimes feared it would never be the same. She had kept up her pretense of being Miss Perfect Christian for her father these past months because she hadn't wanted to hurt him. But now in the muted darkness of the car, mulling his words over in her mind, Raine felt the battle that had raged within her since her mother's passing begin to ease.

She swallowed in the silence, feeling as if someone had poured a soothing balm over a deep wound, balm which would continue to bring healing and peace over time. But it didn't prevent another tear from escaping and running down her face. "But does the . . . hurting ever go away?" she asked softly.

"Not entirely. With God's help we learn to live with it. But it does get easier, and the day comes when we can look back on the good times, the happy memories."

She moved nearer and gave him a hug. "The things you said were . . . very beautiful. Daddy."

"I only pray I was able to help," he said, tightening the embrace before releasing her. "Each of us must learn to deal with grief when it comes our way. Either it makes us press nearer to the God who loves us, or we let it become a wedge that comes between us, stealing the precious relationship we have with Him. He knows our suffering, for He also experienced the deep sadness that comes from the loss of someone very dear. His own innocent Son, after all, took upon Himself the sins of the whole world and died to make our fellowship with His Father possible."

"I never thought about it that way." Raine sighed. "It puts a whole new light on things. I'd like to go home and do some thinking, now."

He patted her knee and started the engine.

During the next several days, Raine kept mostly to herself while she did her chores and ran the house. But in her spare time she stayed in her room, and in the dark of night, she wept into her pillow, venting at last the sorrow she had kept buried for so long behind a facade of strength and peace. Maybe her mother *had* passed on at her appointed time, as it said in the Bible, but nothing could make the pain of missing her go away. Still, Raine began to notice an easing of her bitterness, an acceptance of the loss.

Finally one day Raine knelt before her dresser and opened the bottom drawer. Moving aside a few sweaters, she unearthed a picture frame wrapped in hairpin lace. Even yet a fragrance clung to the fragile shawl. Inhaling delicate lily-of-the-valley memories, Raine gathered it to herself and hugged it as hot tears squeezed past her tightly closed lashes. For several moments she sobbed, rocking the treasure in her arms.

When the tears subsided and the heaviness eased in her heart, she moved to her bed. Turning her eyes to the view outside the window, Raine gingerly undid the wrapping. Then, gathering all of her strength, she allowed her eyes to look at the dear sweet face in the portrait. Surprisingly, her mother's gentle smile brought comfort instead of sorrow, and Raine drank it in thirstily for several minutes. Then, inspired, she took out some drawing paper and charcoals.

Glancing out the window awhile later, she saw a pair of wrens light on a branch high up on the spruce tree. A dollop of new snow that had fallen overnight slipped from the bough and plopped over several more limbs on the way down, collecting even more white before landing on the ground. Raine smiled as the birds flew off. The sun was starting to peek out. It might be a good day for a visit down the lane. Hurriedly she put the new drawing away and went to wash her face. Then she stuffed her sketchbook into her bag and mixed up a batch of brownies.

When Raine reached Dek's place, her mittened knuckles hadn't started knocking on the door before Dek had swung it wide open. With his good side toward her, he took note of her astonished face and gave her an offhand grin. "O'Clancy heard you coming."

"I guess that shouldn't surprise me," she said, ruffling the dog's ears as she stepped inside. "These are for you." Not quite meeting Dek's eyes, she handed him a foil-covered plate.

"Mm. Still warm, even," he said, hiking a corner of the wrapping. He cleared his throat. "Thanks."

Watching as he took them into the kitchen, Raine slipped off her jacket and gloves while she blatantly assessed the living room. The multi-hued braided rug covering most of the wood floor shared complementary shades with the matching oxblood leather furniture. No vases or china nicknacks cluttered about. Just lots of books, mostly hardcover. The fire crackling in the stone fireplace gleamed off three polished rifles inside a built-in gun cabinet and illuminated one of the continents on a stand-mounted globe in one corner of the room. Raine decided against checking out the oil paintings on the walls, just as Dek returned.

"I was about to have some hot chocolate," he said, offering her one of the two mugs he held. He gestured for her to be seated.

"Thank you." Her fingers, uncharacteristically cold from nervousness, wrapped around the hot cup, and she sank into a luxuriously cushiony chair. Raine took a sip, wondering what she was supposed to do next.

"Did you bring any drawings with you?" Dek asked, folding his lanky frame easily into a recliner a bit away from the fireplace. He set down his cup.

"Uh, yes."

"Can I see them?"

Raine expelled a breath she didn't know she'd been holding and fished her sketchbook out of the bag beside her chair. Gingerly she held it out.

Dek put the tablet on his knee and bowed his head over it, averting the damaged side of his face from her view. He opened the cover and perused the first picture. Each page turned slowly during the process while his scarred left hand absently kneaded his forehead.

Raine watched the firelight make glossy patches in his curly hair. The cobalt sweater over his checked shirt looked nice against his coloring, she decided, letting her gaze wander down his denims to a pair of worn western boots. She watched him turn to another sketch as concentration made his brows converge above the bridge of his nose. This was taking an interminably long time, she thought, feeling heat gradually creep up her face. They must be awful. She gulped the rest of her drink and peered despondently into her empty mug. She was hopeless. He was wasting his—

"Not bad," he said glancing up.

"What?"

"You did a great job on these first ones. And the others, well, they're pretty good. You're getting the shading down a lot better."

Raine relaxed somewhat in relief.

"I do have a couple of other comments to make about your work, though."

Her short-lived relief evaporated as she felt her blush coming back full force. Her pulse started to throb. Why had she, novice that she was, come here to this—this expert—and have nerve enough to let him see her amateur chicken scratchings?

"Hey," he said, obviously seeing her distress. "Take it easy. You did want help with these, right?"

Grimly, Raine nodded.

"Well, I told you I won't bite off your head. Do you think I was born knowing everything?"

His unexpected teasing grin put her at ease, and she felt herself relax a fraction. "I guess not. It's just—"

"Yeah, I know. It's hard putting your work out where someone else can see it and pick it apart. I've heard it before and been through it myself."

"Really?"

"Sure. I used to teach art. Come on into the work room," he said, getting up.

Raine rose and followed him through the small, tidy kitchen to a room just beyond. He obviously used it as a studio, with huge windows on two sides and an oversize drafting table in the middle. A profusion of art supplies, magazines, and drawings in various stages filled the shelves along the other walls.

"Have a seat," Dek said, indicating the chair at the drafting table.

As she did, he put her sketchbook in front of her. She swallowed.

Dek filled his lungs slowly and reminded himself that this was a classroom. And he was a professor. Nothing more. He would get through this art lesson smoothly and quickly. He forced himself into his instructing mode just as if this were four years ago and semester classes had just begun.

"There are two things I want to show you today," he said in his teaching role. "You're getting a good hold of shading and how it adds depth to a flat scene. But the other half of it is highlighting. Here, this is what I mean." Reaching over her shoulder, he picked up an eraser. "Of course, this is easier to do in a painting—you'd just add a dab of your lightest color. But it's not totally impossible to do in a pencil sketch. See this shadow right here?"

Conscious of where Dek's arm had brushed hers accidentally, Raine inhaled the clean musk of his aftershave. She forced herself to concentrate on where his finger pointed in the drawing.

"Well. imagine the source of light. It's coming from right about this direction, wouldn't you say?" he said, cupping a simulated shaft of it with his hands. "And if it was strong enough to cause a dark shadow here," he touched a spot on the sketch, "then it would probably hit here and bounce off. Like this." With his burned hand he took the tip of the eraser and started rubbing off a tiny bit of penciled area, then grunted and switched to his right hand.

Raine pretended not to notice. She concentrated on what he did to alter her picture. "I see what you mean," she said with a smile.

Dek saw Raine's face and eyes light up, and despite all his warnings, his breath caught. He'd given himself a hundred lectures about how she was only a kid, and only here in the first place to improve her skill in art. But that glowy face of hers had been taunting him in his dreams, and now her perfume was muddling his thoughts. Maybe this hadn't been such a great idea, doing his Mr. Professor thing again. Did the girl's father approve of her coming down here like this? Did he even know?

"Would it also spark right about here?" she said, breaking into his consciousness.

He cleared his throat. "Uh, yeah. See what you can do with the other sketches." Rubbing his temples, he took a seat across the room to give her the opportunity to work independently. After having been so certain that this part of his life had ended with the accident, it felt great to teach again. Exhilarating, in fact. A raft of faces rose to his mind, faces of eager, would-be artists Dek had put out of his thoughts years ago when he lay recovering in a burn center in Vancouver. Probably most of them had finished their training and gone on into careers of their own, while his had stagnated and drained away, until now.

Then a stronger memory sliced through him with pain that seared at his gut. If only Annie had not been there in the fire. If only none of that night had happened. When she had died, a light had gone out of his life, one he never expected to see illuminate anything in the world again.

With a sigh, he gazed back at Raine deeply engrossed in her work. And he tried not to notice the way she'd brushed one side of her hair back and tucked it behind an ear, leaving the rest of the gleaming red-gold waves to flow over her fragile shoulders.

seven

O'Clancy came padding into the work room and circled himself at his master's feet, settling with his head on his paws while Dek sorted supplies.

Dek saw Raine smile over her shoulder before getting back to her work. "He's nice, quiet company to have around."

"Yeah." *The sum total of all the company I've had for the last three years,* Dek thought grimly. "I got him when he was a pup."

She turned to the previous page and eyed a sketch. "I hope I'm doing this right. You used to teach art, you said?"

Dek nodded, then realizing she couldn't have seen his response, cleared his throat. "Uh, yeah."

"Was that very long ago?"

"A few years. I was an instructor in Banff, at the School of Fine Arts."

"Banff? I was there once."

"That right?"

"Mm hm, when I was a child." She erased a finite bit of charcoal from her drawing and blew trailings away. "We were on furlough, visiting Uncle Shel and Aunt Vi, and they drove us to see the mountains. I remember how beautiful they looked—especially after we'd taken the tram to the top of Sulphur Mountain. I imagine it's all different now."

"It's grown a lot." Dek got up and moved nearer, peering over her arm at her work.

"Is this okay, do you think?"

"Not bad. You catch on pretty quick."

Raine looked up at him, feeling more at ease since the quality of her work apparently satisfied him. "Why aren't you still teaching . . . if you don't mind my asking?"

Breaking eye contact, he turned away with an acrid grimace. Then, shoving his hands into his pockets, he moved to one of the windows and stared out momentarily. "I left after I . . . had my . . . misfortune, shall we say," he grated. "After that I was busy getting put back together."

"I . . . I'm sorry. I didn't mean to pry."

He shrugged nonchalantly, and when he spoke again his voice had lost much of its bitter tone. "It's all over and done with. No way to change the past."

Who knew that more than she? Raine wondered. She could never go back to Haiti and have things be the same as they'd been when her mom was alive. Sneaking a glance at Dek, she noticed a resigned droop to his shoulders, and wished she'd kept her mouth shut. "Sometimes . . . it's hard to understand why God allows—"

"Do me a favor, would you?" he said evenly. "This is an art lesson, not a Sunday school. I'm not interested in the mysterious workings of the Almighty."

Raine felt as though she'd been slapped. Warmth spread over her face as his words echoed in her ears. "*Ka poul bwe dlo, li pa blie Bo-Die,*" she muttered to herself.

"What was that?"

"Nothing. Just a popular saying in Haiti." Feeling his challenging stare, she lifted her chin. "It means, 'When a chicken drinks water it doesn't forget to raise its head in thanks to God.' "

A scowl narrowed his dark eyes, but he did not respond. Raine dropped her stare and switched her attention to her work, finishing in heavy silence. "That's the last one."

Dek crossed the space separating them and bent to inspect the sketches. He shouldn't have been so sharp with her. He knew that. After all, he hadn't wanted to hurt her feelings. The sight of her lowered lashes and flushed cheeks made him feel as though someone had gouged his insides with a dull palette knife. He let out an exasperated breath. "Look, I'm sorry. I didn't mean to—"

"No, I'm the one who should apologize. Forgive me."

Dek held her gaze for a few seconds.

Finally she looked away. The barest hint of a smile curved her mouth.

He shook his head. At least she didn't hold grudges, he thought. But they'd delved deeply enough into things personal. It was time to get back to business. He raked his fingers through his hair. "Well, I guess we should move on to the second part of the lesson."

With the easing of tension, relief washed over Raine. She nibbled her lower lip and raised her brows. "Which is?"

"Viewpoint."

"Viewpoint. What is that?"

He flipped back a few pages in her sketchbook to a scene she'd drawn of the woodland pond. "See this?"

"Mm hm. You said the shading is right, and you also approved the highlighting. What's the matter with it then?"

He didn't answer.

"Viewpoint? Well, why don't you tell me what it is, for heaven's sake? Oh, excuse me. I mean for Pete's sake."

Dek rolled his eyes. "Now don't get facetious on me. Just look at it for a minute."

Frowning, Raine tilted her head and stared at the sketch. "It's wrong?"

"No, not exactly. It's good. But it could be better. I'll show you." Moving to the shelves, he pulled out an assortment of cut photo mats and chose one with a five-inch by seven-inch opening. He positioned it over a section of her sketch, shutting off the surrounding portion. He watched her study it. "See any difference?"

"Now that you mention it, yes. It looks better."

"Know why? Because you've just eliminated the part that detracted from the meat of the composition. A sketch should show its heart, the part that appealed to you in the first place. Any more is only fluff."

"I'd never thought about it that way before, but you're right."

He picked a small object out of a bin of assorted odds and ends and handed it to her. "Here. I used to give these to my students to help them find the heart of a scene. You might find it useful."

Raine looked at the empty slide casing and held it a few inches from her face, then peered through it with one eye. "Yes, this is great. Thank you." Noticing her watch just then, she checked the hour. "Goodness, I've used up your whole afternoon. I didn't mean to impose on you so long."

"I wasn't busy."

She nodded. "Well, I . . . um . . . I need to know how I should pay for the instruction. I really don't expect you to do all this for nothing."

"It's not exactly a formal lesson, you know. No grade, no credit."

"But it's still taking up your time, and I appreciate your help."

"Friends don't put price tags on things, now, do they?"

Smiling into his eyes. Raine shrugged. "No, I guess not."

"Then let's just keep it that way."

While brushing her hair later that night, Raine reflected on her art lesson. Dek had an easygoing method of teaching that made complicated procedures extremely simple. But still, he'd been somewhat ill at ease, tending to keep his damaged side averted from her. Truth was, she barely noticed his scars until he drew attention to them. She wished he would stop trying to hide. There had been a few times when she'd caught brief glimpses of a very appealing quality in him—a flash of humor. But almost as soon as it would appear, he'd close it off and become the stilted professor again.

Professor Decker. She tried to picture him before a class of bright young students. No doubt it had been difficult for most of the girls to concentrate on what he said, when they probably were more interested in feasting their eyes and hoping he'd be the model during their life studies term. He'd turn any woman's head, even now.

What had happened to him? Whatever it was, it had taken place only a few years ago. She still cringed at the bitterness in his tone when she'd tried to draw him out. Not that his past was any of her business, but she couldn't help but wonder about the accident. Talking things out was supposed to accelerate a person's healing process. At least it seemed to be working for her, now that she'd talked to her father. Perhaps in time Dek, too, would open up.

But the way he blamed God for it hit home. She had felt the same about her own circumstances until a few short nights ago. All her life she'd been told that all things work together for good, but she could think of no way that that truth could apply to burns. And she felt hopelessly inadequate for the particular task of smoothing Dek's way to God. With that grim thought, she undressed.

Heading for the car with her father after church that Sunday, Raine heard swift footsteps behind them. She turned.

"Oh, Lorraine," Steve called. "I meant to ask you something, but didn't get the chance. I was wondering if you'd consider spending the day in town with me. You don't mind, do you Lucas?" he said, with a quick glance at her father.

"Not at all. I can pick her up tonight when I come in for the service."

"Wait just a minute, you two," Raine said, looking from one to the other. "I haven't agreed to anything just yet."

"Sorry, I should have explained," the minister said. "I need to make a few calls this afternoon on some single-parent moms, and it goes a lot smoother if I have another woman along."

"Oh, really?"

"Yes." He slid a hand casually into his slacks pocket. "Usually Francie comes with me, but she's home with a sore throat. You wouldn't have to talk or anything, if you didn't want to."

"I see. Well, in that case, I suppose I wouldn't mind helping out."

"Excellent. I'll just lock up all the doors and meet you at my car in a few minutes." He unfastened a pair of keys from a ring and held them out.

She closed her gloved hand over them and watched him walk back to the church. Slanting a gaze toward her father, she saw his confident expression. "I wish you'd let me accept my own invitations, Daddy."

He chuckled.

"And don't make so much of things. I'll see you later," she said, then walked to Steve's Buick.

By the time the day ended, Raine had a fair appreciation for the duties of a pastor, plus a healthy respect for his tact in varied situations. Even though she had been along chiefly for the ride, she felt worn out at the thought of carrying so many people's burdens, as Steven seemed to do with ease and genuine sincerity.

On their way back to the church, she felt his gaze and looked up to meet it.

"Something wrong?" he inquired.

"Why do you ask?"

"I don't know. You seem preoccupied or something."

Her thoughts reflected on the incredible ease with which Steven coaxed people to discuss their innermost heartaches. Would she ever be able to get Dek to open up to her? She wanted that so much. "I met someone who sort of needs help, and I don't know how to reach him . . . especially since I've been facing some difficult things myself and am only beginning to work through them."

"Well, I've found out quite often that when we make an effort to ease someone else's burdens, our own begin to lighten. Sometimes the only thing we can do is pray. But if you ever feel the need to talk . . .".

"I know. Come to the pastor."

With a chuckle, Steven shook his head. "Hey, pastors can also be friends, you know. And once in awhile, even more."

Raine blushed. She was glad there wasn't daylight enough for it to show. She decided to switch to a safer topic. "The advice you gave Tricia Harding was really good, you know. You're a natural at counseling."

"It's just one of my many talents," he teased.

"No, really," she said, determined to keep things casual. "I mean it. It's hard to try to raise babies alone in this world. Encouraging her to start a support group with some of her friends was brilliant. Could be the turning point in her life."

"Well, a person can't help but notice how low her self-esteem is at the moment. Having someone you count on walk out on you without warning really puts a hole in your confidence."

"I would imagine. Do you think there's still hope for that marriage?"

Steven paused as if in thought. "Well, there's always hope. There had to be some feeling between them to have gotten married in the first place, wouldn't you think?"

"You're probably right."

"Sure, little kids put a strain on a relationship, and all that," he went on. "But still, a husband and wife can talk things out and come up with some sort of compromise. The hard thing in that circumstance is the husband's unbelief. An 'unequal yoke,' as the Bible calls it. Makes for two entirely different perspectives. A Christian is only asking for trouble in a relationship with an unbeliever."

Thinking about his comments, Raine glanced out the window, trying to ease the twinge of guilt that was making its discomforting presence known inside her. Then she turned back. "Now that I've had the chance to see you in action, you might say, I couldn't help but notice how easily you work spiritual things into a conversation."

He smiled. "I almost said that's my job, then caught myself. I guess it's closer to the truth to say it's my life."

"Know what? I believe you."

"Do you find it hard to share your faith, Lorraine?"

She thought of the past ten months of her life and the way grief had taken a chunk out of her foundation, leaving a void, a hollow place. Even now that she had begun to recover she doubted there could possibly be anything left in her that would be of help to anyone else. She couldn't even meet Steven's eyes.

"Well, if you ever need anybody to listen, remember I'm here. Okay?" Steve said.

"I will."

Raine didn't wait until she got back from the mailbox to tear open Sarah's letter a few days later. Eagerly she drew out the folded pages and devoured them.

> *Hi, You,*
>
> *Just finished up my hours at the clinic office and thought I'd scribble a few lines your way. You sounded ever so lonesome in your last letter. I've finally convinced Dad that a visit would benefit both of us, so I'll be there for a few weeks in December . . . hope that's okay. I expect to arrive on the first.*
>
> *I'm so looking forward to it! Just the thought of having days and days to do nothing but visit will be heaven. And you know how I love horses. It'll be like that summer we spent in England with my Auntie Maeve on the horse breeding farm that once was our home. We'll have a grand time.*
>
> *Hope I'll get to meet that secretive neighbor of*

yours. He sounds fascinating. Any other prospects around, or is he the only available male for miles?

Well, it's quite late, so I shall make this short. It's far better to talk anyway. Letters are so one-sided.

> *See you soon. Love,*
> *Me*

Raine hugged the letter to herself and almost skipped the rest of the way. "Daddy!" she called as she hung her jacket on the rack. "Sarah's coming!"

Her father looked up from the book he was reading. "That *is* good news. When will she be here?"

"First of December, she says. That's just a few weeks away. I'll have to get the extra room freshened up and ready for her. I am so happy!"

Raine's enthusiasm spilled over onto everything during the next several days as she washed and aired linens and helped her father paper one wall of Sarah's room. She hoped the lavender quilted spread she'd ordered from the Sears catalog would bring out the delicate orchid floral pattern of the wallpaper. In her leisure moments during the day—and even during long hours of the night as she lay awake—she found herself imagining the good times ahead for Sarah and herself.

Finally, in a desperate attempt to get rid of excess energy, she baked some chocolate chip cookies and went the entire length of the lane on foot to deliver them to Alan Decker.

His surprise when he answered the door filled her with chagrin as he cast a scathing look down at the grungy sweatshirt he wore. "Raine. I wasn't expecting you."

She smiled. "Does that mean I have to walk all the way back home?"

"You walked here?" he said, shaking his head in amazement. "Well, in that case, be my guest." He stepped aside, gesturing for her to come in.

"Thank you. I baked these today." She held out a foil-wrapped plate.

Taking it, Dek grinned. "Thanks." He removed a cookie and took a bite. "Mm. Trying to fatten me up, huh? Not that I mind, you understand. These are my favorites."

Pleased, she smiled.

"Bring any sketches with you?" he asked.

"No. I've been too busy. I thought maybe I'd learn as much by checking out your paintings instead." She averted his gaze. "But now that I said that, it sounds stupid."

He finished the last half of his cookie and swallowed. "Well, I'm not Van Gogh, you know. But feel free to look them over. I'll put on some coffee."

"Dek?" she said to his departing back.

He stopped and turned.

"Thank you. I really just wanted to visit. I'm glad you didn't throw me out." Unzipping her jacket, she hung it on the doorknob, then wandered about the room scrutinizing the oils on display.

He came back shortly with two steaming mugs. Placing one beside Raine as she warmed herself at the fire, Dek took his usual seat.

"Have you decided anything about my incredible talent?" he asked wryly.

She met his brown eyes. "Yes. You do rather well with wildlife. I've never had any success with animals. They don't hold still long enough."

"That's why *you* have to remain still, taking note of as much as you can. I have some books on animal anatomy you can borrow sometime, if you like."

"That would be nice."

Dek studied Raine's features as the flames on the hearth glowed over her ivory skin and tipped her long lashes with gold. She was on some other channel today. Not here to discuss art. "Why did you come?"

One of her shoulders shrugged slightly beneath her sky blue fleece shirt. "I needed to get out of the house."

"Problems?"

She smiled and met his gaze. "No. Antsy. My best friend from Haiti, Sarah Hamilton, is coming for a visit the first of December. I've been getting a room ready for her, and suddenly I couldn't stand home there another minute."

With a sigh, he looked away. "Well, that'll be . . . nice." That's all he needed. Another stranger. He was just beginning to get used to Raine. He hoped she didn't plan on bringing this Sarah person along on future visits or lessons. He took a gulp of coffee. In all likelihood Raine would be too busy for art instruction once her company arrived. He didn't analyze the unexpected feeling of disappointment that coursed through his veins with that realization. But it rankled him. Gripping his mug, he drained it.

Raine finished her drink, then rose. "Well, I'd better head home. I have to make sure Daddy's packed enough clothes for the retreat in Edmonton tomorrow. Thanks for the coffee."

"Sure."

"I hope it'll be okay to bring Sarah to meet you," Raine said. "She's sweet. You'll like her."

"We'll see," Dek answered, walking Raine to the door. The first of December. That was hardly more than a week away.

eight

Relief filled Raine as she hung up the phone. The new bed-spread for Sarah's room had arrived at the catalog store in town. As soon as her father returned, they would be able to pick it up and get in extra groceries. Her footsteps echoed in the empty house as she went to the kitchen for a cup of tea. She walked to the front window and peered out as she sipped her drink.

Storm and Buckwheat stood with their bodies touching in the bitter cold, puffs of air from their nostrils joining together in a splotch of moist whiteness. All over the bleak landscape, occasional patches of spruce added areas of dark green among the barren trees and bushes.

Against the white of winter, the worn fence and gate looked especially dismal with their chipped paint and broken or missing boards—nothing like the way Uncle Sheldon had kept them years ago. The place had looked so pretty then, especially with Aunt Violet's geraniums and petunias growing in profusion. Perhaps in the spring Daddy would feel up to doing some outside repairs. With a sigh, Raine turned away.

Crossing to the fireplace, she added a log to the blaze, then curled up on the couch with a mystery novel she'd started a few nights before. Fairly certain she'd already figured out the identity of the guilty party, she plugged along just to be sure.

In the middle of a particularly tense paragraph the phone rang, jarring her. She drew a calming breath and closed the book over her finger, then picked up the receiver. "Hello?"

"Those are brownies I smell, right?" came Dek's deep voice.

"I beg your pardon?" A smile spread across Raine's face.

"Yeah. I went outside for something, and that unmistakable smell floated my way. Figured it had to be from your place. This is Dek."

"I already knew that."

"Did you?"

"Of course."

"So, am I right?"

Raine laughed lightly. "You're hungry? That's why you called?"

"Well," he hedged, his tone becoming more serious, "actually I'm just checking up on you, since you said your father was going away. Everything okay?"

An unexpected warmth washed over her. Only a moment ago she had felt completely alone in the world. "Yes. Thanks. I was already starting to talk to the walls, though. I didn't realize this house was so big."

"Yeah, well, you'll probably get used to it. How long will you be left high and dry, anyway?"

"Just till the day after tomorrow, but my dad didn't take the car. So I'm only technically stranded."

"How's that?"

"I can't drive."

Dek sputtered into a laugh. "You're joking."

"No. I just never had the occasion to learn. We didn't have our own vehicle in Haiti, only a van everyone shared as needed." That sounded bizarre even to Raine as she set down her book and twisted her finger in the coils of the receiver cord.

"Are the keys there?"

"Probably. Why?"

"Why do you think? I have skills in fields other than art. It's about time you learn how to drive."

"Now you're the one who's joking. It's all snowy outside. Icy.

Slippery."

"It's not that bad," he returned. "This is Canada, you know. Snow rarely keeps people from going places."

"All the same . . ."

"Oh. There it is again."

"There's what again?"

"Essence of chocolate. Another wave of it. They almost done?"

Raine laughed again and unentwined her fingers from the wire. "Tell you what. Give me about an hour, and I'll whip some up. Good enough?"

"Perfect. Lunchtime. I'll bring the mooseburgers."

"What?" she gasped.

"Nothing like 'em. See you in awhile."

Before Raine could formulate a reply, the line clicked and went dead. Replacing the receiver on its cradle, she schooled herself to be calm. For some reason Alan Decker sounded like he was in the best mood she'd encountered so far. And oddly enough, she felt certain it was closer to his real self than was the stiff, guarded person he tried so hard to make seem convincing. This could turn out to be a very interesting day. But really, mooseburgers? She dashed to her room to run a brush through her hair.

Dek gave O'Clancy a slightly embarrassed shrug. "Just making sure she's okay, that's all. She's not used to being on her own. I'm merely being, in her word, neighborly." No harm in that, he told himself for the tenth time. After all, soon enough that friend of hers would be underfoot, and Raine would be too busy for lessons or visits. But all else aside, she should know how to drive. Until she had mentioned that, going to see her was the furthest thing from his mind. The absolute furthest, he assured himself.

Half an hour later, he pulled through the gate of Misty Hills Ranch and brought the Bronco to a stop in front of the walk. Up close, the whole place looked like it could use a coat of paint. Except the house. The white aluminum siding and forest green shutters were quite attractive against the red shingled roof. He got out and pressed the doorbell.

In moments the door opened, and Raine smiled from the other side of it, her hair shiny and softly curled around that guileless face. He tried not to notice that her purple and white velour sweats made her look small and fragile. Or that her fair coloring seemed even more delicate under an alluring rosy flush.

"Hi," she said. "Come on in."

With a nod, he followed her up the breezeway steps and into the house. Entering the kitchen, he gave the three rooms in view a quick once-over as he unzipped his jacket and hung it on the rack just inside the door. The interior seemed in good repair. Rich pine paneling, fairly new appliances, fine quality furniture—even if a bit sparse. No excess of vases or useless decorations. He slid a sideways glance at Raine and inhaled exaggeratedly with a disarming grin. "See? Didn't I tell you? Chocolate. It's addicting, you know."

Raine's lips gaped with a disbelieving shake of her head.

"Hey, it's true," he said in mock seriousness. "Up till this fall I rarely ever ate the stuff. Now I seem to need a fix every couple days, or I go all funny."

"Yes, I see that."

Her skepticism put a sparkle in her eyes that looked somehow at home there, Dek decided. He held out the paper bag he'd brought with him.

She took it with some hesitance and peered inside. "Thanks.

I've, um, never made these before." She lifted her lashes. "Do people really eat moose?"

"Nothing but." He winked. "If you steer me to your broiler, I'll take care of them. Fair enough?"

She nodded.

While he broiled the ground moose patties, Raine threw some frozen french fries into the oven and set two places at the table, managing to stay out of Dek's way while he clanged pans about.

"Smells delicious," Raine said as they sat down to eat. "Did you . . . shoot it?"

"What?"

"The moose."

"Oh, no. Gift from a friend who likes to hunt." He picked up his burger and gestured for her to start.

Raine moistened her lips. Then after nibbling the lower one uncertainly, she bowed her head and said a quick silent prayer.

Dek cleared his throat and averted his gaze while he poured ketchup on his fries. He would have been more surprised if she'd have foregone that obvious custom, now that he thought about it.

She straightened and picked up her burger. Throwing caution aside, she took a healthy bite. "Know something?" she said after she swallowed. "This isn't half bad."

They both broke into laughter.

After lunch things had been cleared away, they bundled up and went out to the garage.

"Okay," Dek said as they got into the car. "The left pedal is the clutch. The middle one is the brake. That long one's the accelerator. It's the clutch that's likely to give you the most trouble."

"Why does the car have one?" Raine asked gripping the

steering wheel, a perplexed expression clouding her face. "I've never even seen a clutch before."

"Well, some people prefer to shift gears for themselves. Anyway, first thing you do is depress the clutch and move the gear shift to neutral, then turn the key."

"Where's neutral?"

Her question would have sounded ludicrous had her expression not been so innocent and sincere. This lesson would present far more challenge than would any aspect of art she needed to learn. He opened his door, got out, and strode around the car. "Switch places. I'll show you what I mean."

Once settled in again, Raine concentrated hard on everything he was showing her as he took the car out and made several slow-motion demonstrations back and forth in the front drive. It looked easy enough. But when her turn came, she found her only talent seemed to lie in stalling the engine—and that after severe bucking and grinding of the gears. She moaned in frustration. "Are you sure you want to do this? I hate it!"

"Sure. You'll get the hang of it. You'll see."

"This isn't even legal, is it? Don't I need some kind of permit or something?"

Dek knew she was stalling. He steeled himself against her pleading tone as he habitually turned his collar up over his scars. "Not on your own property. Once you can handle driving around the place, you can get a learner's permit and start practicing on the road."

"Oh."

"Come on," he said patiently. "Give it another try."

With a determined sigh, Raine gritted her teeth and eased the car forward ever so slowly. Filled with elation at her small success, she smiled in triumph. Her strangle hold on the steering wheel eased.

"That's it. You're getting it. Now, stop and start a few more times, and we'll move on to second gear."

"Hey, this is really fun," she said sometime later as she braked to a stop after a couple dozen passes between the outbuildings and the lane. "I'm beginning to like it."

Dek chuckled to himself, then only barely swallowed a laugh when she stalled the car again and shot him a glare. "Concentrate."

"Yes, professor," she spat. But the twinkle in her eyes more than tempered her tone as she started the motor and drove the length of the drive, then back again. She cautiously guided the car into the big old garage and turned off the key. "Won't Daddy be surprised. Of course, I won't tell him until I'm better at it."

"That comes pretty quick with practice. You did a good job today—especially considering it was only your first time." Dek checked his watch and got out. "Well, I'd better be heading home before it gets too late."

"I can't believe how quickly the afternoon passed," she said, joining him for the walk back to the house. "Thank you, Dek, for taking the time to—" Her heel caught on a root, sending her into a very undignified headfirst sprawl in the snow. A sharp jab shot through her as her rib connected with a concealed rock. She bit back a moan.

On reflex, Dek grabbed her and stood her up, a look of concern wrinkling his brow as he held her at arm's length. "You okay?"

Nodding, Raine turned a brilliant shade of red as she ignored the sore spot and brushed snow off herself. "Well, so much for my dreams of becoming a world-class ballerina, huh? What a klutz." Her laugh, airy and light, echoed in the stillness.

It brought a low, answering one rumbling from deep inside

Dek, and without thinking, he drew her close and wrapped his arms around her. "You are something else," he said in wonder.

Raine shut her eyes for a few seconds, her cheek against the cool surface of his leather jacket as a wave of pain ebbed. How long had it been since anyone besides her father had held her? She had missed at least a thousand hugs since they'd left Haiti. But slowly the realization of where she was made its way into her consciousness. Her pulse began to pick up. She cleared her throat and eased away, suddenly afraid to meet Dek's eyes. If he apologized she'd die.

He paused but a heartbeat before lifting her chin with the edge of his fingers as though it were the most natural thing in the world for a person to do. "Sure you're not hurt?"

She nodded and expended great effort to make sure her voice came out evenly. "Just my dignity. The Lord likes to keep people humble."

Frowning, he tipped his head and studied her.

"It was all that over-confidence from my great driving," she elaborated, hoping to restore their easy camaraderie.

"More like the kind of 'time and chance that happen to all of us,' " he quipped wryly.

Raine's mouth dropped open, and she shot him an astonished look. "Was that actually Scripture you were spouting, Alan Decker? I am impressed."

A sudden reddish glow rose from his neck and tinted his good ear as he shifted his stance and started striding toward the Bronco. "Yeah, well, I never said I couldn't read. I said I was uninterested."

"Oh. I forgot." With a few quick steps after him, she managed to catch up.

But forgetting what Dek had said was about the last thing Raine would ever do. After straightening up the house for the night, she opened a can of soup and heated it in the microwave, then sat down to eat it as her mind replayed the day's events. She had expected the only human voice she'd hear while her father was in Edmonton would be her own, talking to the horses in the morning and again at night. She thought she'd be so at loose ends by noon she would resort to giving Uncle Sheldon's old television a swift kick to see if perhaps the set would turn on. If anyone would have asked her to name the most unlikely thing that might transpire that day, she would have said having Dek come by, that is if she'd have thought such a thing could happen in a million years.

Alan Decker was incredible. Despite the energy he put into appearing reserved and self-sufficient and uncaring, his facade was slipping. He was warm and witty and spontaneous. Helpful. Strong. When he had rescued her in the forest some weeks ago, he had pulled her onto his horse as though she were little more than a feather. And today when he'd helped her up and then hugged her, she'd felt secure in his arms, as though nothing could ever hurt her there. She could still feel the smooth leather jacket against her face, the solid chest beneath it.

Raine closed her eyes and wrapped herself in the warm memory for an extended moment. When she had first met Dek, she thought he needed a friend. She'd thought *she* needed a friend back then, too. But what about now? Was friendship what she truly wanted?

She shifted uncomfortably trying to ease her bruised rib, then drew a shallow breath so it wouldn't hurt.

At home, Dek ground his teeth together. Jerk. Fool. Nincompoop. What had possessed him to put his arms around Raine? She'd be getting all kinds of wrong ideas. *He'd* be getting all kinds of wrong ideas. Sure, she was alone, and he wanted to be sure she was okay up there. But the phone call had been sufficient, and if he'd left it at that there wouldn't have been any messy complications.

He should have tried harder to send her away in the very beginning, nipped things in the bud when she first started coming around. He pressed his mouth into a thin line. What was there about Raine Montrose that made him take leave of his senses? She was a kid. A kid just like so many others he'd taught in college. Well, he admitted, not quite. She really wanted to master art, not just "find herself." There seemed nothing superficial about her. She was too trusting, too honest. And would be easily hurt by someone who wanted to take advantage of her. If she had any sense, she'd start running now and never stop.

He had been better off before she pointed that little freckled nose his way. Things were fine then. Yeah. Just fine, he huffed. Clancy's a great conversationalist. Wonderful company, too. And he never reminded Dek of what life was like before. When he had Annie.

Annie's slender, lithe form danced in his memory, fringed lashes surrounding wide brown eyes, her short cap of chestnut hair like silk to the touch. Her hands which had fashioned intricate sculptures had felt tender, warm. He had known her almost from the first day he had arrived in Banff after hitchhiking from Toronto. Working as a waitress to pay her way through art school, her interest in art complemented his. When they finally married, they'd been deeply happy and thought it would go on forever.

But there had been no forever for them. Out of the blue, God had taken her away—and people said God was love. Dek had even believed that once himself, a long time ago. But no more. When Annie died, part of him died, too. Now he had no use for religion. It was for fools. A band of pain tightened inside his chest.

He should never have gone out that night without Annie. He should have heeded that feeling that things weren't quite right. But he'd let her convince him to go to the exhibit and support his students' work. A last peck on her feverish cheek, a gentle smile . . . and that was the last picture his mind carried of her.

Now it was fading a little more each day, growing fuzzy and obscure, stealing from his memory the qualities that had drawn him to her so many years ago. Already he was forgetting things. The sound of her voice, the shape of her face. What kind of husband would forget those kinds of details?

The weight of guilt grew heavier, and Dek shut his eyelids against the pressure. If only he had told her that night how much he loved her. He inhaled deeply and forced himself to relax. He didn't deserve anything but a solitary life. Loneliness was fit punishment for a failure. The emergency crew should never have dragged him out of the house. There was no reason for him to still be alive. None at all. He had nothing to give anyone.

At least, not until Raine Montrose had come stumbling across his place. His thoughts settled upon her tranquil green eyes. Deep and probing, they were. The kind that could see past a person's defenses, beyond imperfections. Innocent eyes. She was like the first fragile raindrops after an eternity of drought. And she brought warmth and life his way with her friendship. Made him feel like a human again.

Made him feel a whole lot of things.

And what was she? A missionary kid. A person who had spent every single year of her life learning about God and passing on that knowledge at every opportunity. Some unlikely pair they'd make.

Perhaps Raine wasn't the only one who should start running.

nine

The following morning passed at a turtle's pace as Raine made a circuit in the house, straightening neat rooms, sweeping floors already clear of dust, trying to avoid looking at the phone, and wondering if Dek would call again. Surely he wouldn't, she told herself, and she'd get by just fine. But still it would be nice if he did, her other self argued. Maybe the phone wasn't even working. After all, there had been a snowstorm during the night. Moving to it, she picked up the receiver and listened to the drone of the dial tone. With a guilty grimace, she replaced it on the cradle. And just then it rang.

Raine jumped. Placing a hand to her throat to calm herself, she answered on the second ring. "Hello?"

"Hi, honey. It's Dad. Things okay at home?"

"Yes, fine, Daddy," she said as reality brought her gently back to earth. "How's the retreat going?"

"Good, good. Speakers, food, even the company. Having a great time."

"I'm glad."

"I couldn't help wondering how you were getting by, though, on that big place all by yourself."

Raine recalled the day before, and guilt subdued the smile that was trying so hard to break forth. She could easily say she hadn't been altogether alone. "Oh, everything's okay here. I miss you, though."

"Yeah, me, too. Well, take care. I'll be home late tomorrow."

"Okay. See you." As she hung up, Raine hated herself for not mentioning Alan Decker. But she had no doubts that her relationship with someone who had absolutely no use for God would not meet with her dad's favor. Otherwise she would have told him weeks ago that someone had rescued her that night she had been left in the woods, and that ever since then she'd been calling on that man, arranging art lessons, taking him things to eat, and cultivating his friendship. Perhaps even more. The last thought stabbed at her conscience, and she hoped fervently that Dek would not call again—at least for a little while. Until things could go back to the way they were before.

If she had any sense, she'd go along with her father's unspoken—but quite obvious—hope that she and Steven Grogan might form a relationship. Steve was easily the sort of person her father would choose for her. Open, honest, resourceful, and ever so eligible. He and her father already shared a deep respect and enjoyed being around one another. He was a caring, giving, unselfish young man. But Raine had always believed that when the right man came across her path she'd know. And what she knew about Steven was that he wasn't the right one. She just didn't know why. Before getting into a complex debate about the issue, Raine went to fix herself a sandwich.

Dek smoothed the surface of a new door he'd been making for his work room cabinet, then held it away to study it. He picked up the plane and ran it one more time along an upper corner as fragrant wood shavings dropped in curls around his boots. That would probably do it, he decided, reaching for the sandpaper and running it lightly over the new edge. He'd hoped the job would take him all day to complete, keep him too busy to have time on his hands, but all there was left to do was put on the hinges and fasten the thing in place. And it was barely two o'clock. Picking up a screwdriver, he carried the cabinet door up the basement steps.

Just as he put in the last screw, Dek's stomach growled. At least he'd eliminated the possibility of inviting himself for lunch this time, he told himself smugly. Raine had probably eaten hours ago. At that thought, a few memories he'd managed to keep a lid on surfaced—of her delightful surprise at the first taste of mooseburgers and the sheer determination she'd used to conquer the clutch of her father's car. Had that been only yesterday? It seemed longer.

He idly tapped a finger and cast a look toward the ceiling. Okay, okay. In a little while, after he cleaned up the mess downstairs and had some lunch, then he'd make one very short phone call to make sure she was all right. But that's it. No idle chatter, no more complications, no more hearing that sparkly laugh of hers, and definitely no more getting talked into going back there. He bounded down the basement steps three at a time and had the place in order in less than ten minutes. Then after swallowing a ham sandwich practically whole and scorching his throat gulping hot coffee, he barely missed stepping on Clancy's sleeping form on his way to the phone.

"Hello?" came her voice after the first ring.

Dek hesitated, then cleared his throat. "Hi. Just checking in with you again."

"Oh. Dek. Nice of you to call."

"Everything okay up there?"

"Yes. Everything's fine. Quiet."

Reclining his chair back, Dek relaxed. "Practice any driving today?"

Her light laugh skimmed over the wire, then caught abruptly. "Raine?"

"I'm fine," she rasped. "I just moved the wrong way, and it hurt my side for a second."

"Your side?"

"It's nothing. Just a bruise from my little tumble yesterday. Nothing to worry about."

He frowned. "I thought you said you weren't hurt."

"Well, it was just a little thing. No big deal."

"Not at the time, maybe. But if it's still hurting today—" An alarming picture of her in a body cast and in traction flashed into his mind.

"I'm fine. Really. So how's your day?" she asked, her tone casual.

"Quiet. Slow." *Bordering on dead*, he added silently. "I've been down in my workshop most of the time."

"Oh."

"How about yours?"

She chuckled. "Just taking it easy, actually, trying to get a bit more done on a sketch I wanted to give to my father for Christmas. But it's a little beyond me, I think."

"What's the subject?"

"I'm trying to copy a portrait of my mother. But I'm about ready to forget the whole idea."

"I, uh, have a good book on portraits," he began. Shut up, an inner voice ordered. Now.

"Oh, really?"

"Right. I could, uh, bring it by." He felt his lungs deflate all at once as a few resolutions taunted his mind. No idle chatter. No getting talked into going up there. "Can't stay, though," he blurted quickly.

"Oh, I wouldn't want to put you out, if you're busy."

"No. It's okay. No trouble at all. I'll be there in a few minutes."

Raine hung up the phone, then opened the kitchen door and began fanning a dishtowel in that direction, hoping the aroma of the chocolate chip cookies she had baked a little while ago would permeate the breezeway. Caught suddenly by the extent of her own deviousness, she laughed, then grabbed her side with a wince. *He said he couldn't stay, remember? Don't be so dumb.*

As she hung the towel on the rack, the sound of Dek's car carried from the drive. She went to greet him.

He looked guarded as he approached, as if he had a lot on his mind. But a half grin turned his expression friendly, and just a touch sheepish.

"Hi," she said, with her brightest smile.

He nodded, then inhaled, looking beyond her, the hardcover book dangling at his side.

She lowered her gaze to it.

"Oh. Here."

She closed her fingers around it as he held it out. "Thank you. I, um, have some coffee on," she said tentatively.

"I . . . guess one cup wouldn't hurt."

"Oh. Well, come on in."

As Dek took a seat at the table, Raine filled two cups and joined him, noticing that the appreciative glance he slid over the plate of cookies continued on and included her. She was glad she'd put on her sapphire sweater and gray wool slacks that morning. Moistening her lips, she took a sip of her drink. "I didn't think you'd come today."

"Yeah, well, I hadn't planned on it. I was busy."

"So you said."

"Is that sketch handy that you were working on?" he asked casually, biting into a cookie. "Since I'm here, I might as well be of help."

She flushed at the unexpected offer. "Yes, but I don't think it's good enough for you to see. It's kind of an experiment. It's only—"

"Raine, just get the drawing, will you?" Light exasperation colored his tone.

She rose, holding her arm close to her sore rib as she crossed to the couch and picked up her sketchbook. Already open to the right page, she set it and the photograph in front of him and took her chair again while he compared them.

He finally looked up. "Your mother was quite beautiful. You favor her, you know."

Raine's heart skipped a beat at the compliment. "Thank you."

"You must miss her."

"You're right. I do." *More than I can even say*, her mind continued as sudden tears stung her eyes. She blinked quickly and swallowed. She wanted so much to talk about her mom to someone, but knew she could not speak over the lump in her throat. Averting her gaze, she forced her thoughts elsewhere.

As if out of consideration for her obvious sorrow, Dek transferred his attention to the sketch again. "I see why you're having problems," he went on simply. "Some of your proportions are off a little. I'll show you what I mean. Where'd you put the book?"

Dek watched Raine walk gracefully across the kitchen and retrieve the text. No wonder those soft green eyes seemed always to shimmer, with tears from her recent loss lurking so near. He knew exactly how she felt, recalling how at sixteen he'd lost his own widowed mother. It was the last time he had ever cried. Even after his own accident and Annie's death he'd kept himself under tight control. His admiration for Raine's thoughtfulness in not prying into his own private pain rose a notch.

Right about then he realized how hard it was becoming to keep those things buried inside, and that if Raine were to ask, he'd tell her anything she wanted to know. Shifting uncomfortably in his seat, he accepted the book and slipped into his teaching persona.

By the time the lesson was over, Raine felt far more hopeful about her ability to finish the picture for her father. She was even looking forward to getting back to work on it as soon as Dek left. Hopefully she hadn't taken up too much of his time. She stood and glanced absently at the clock. "Good heavens," she gasped. "It's after five already. Might I . . . offer you some supper?"

Dek's thick dark brows rose as an easy smile spread across his mouth. "I appreciate the invitation. but no, thanks. I'd better be on my way." He got up and pushed in his chair. Removing his jacket from the rack, he turned with a grin as he pulled it on. "Thanks for the coffee and cookies.".

"Oh, let me send some home with you," she said, dashing to the counter.

"You don't have to," he began, then stopped as Raine filled a foil pie tin with them and returned.

"I wouldn't want you to get the shakes." she teased, holding them out.

He stared at her long and hard. A strange light showed in his deep-set eyes as a smile played at the corners of his mouth. "You are unbelievable, know that? And I do thank you for these." Accepting her offering, his fingers brushed hers. With the hint of a wink, he left.

As his truck pulled away, Raine leaned back against the kitchen door and closed her eyes, still tingling from his touch. She released all her breath at once. The house seemed twice as large now. Not quite ready to face the lonely echoes, she grabbed her coat and went out to feed the horses.

Part way there, a slow realization made its way past the quickened beating of her heart. Alan Decker had not tried to hide his scars even once that day. And she hadn't noticed them at all.

Against her better judgment the next afternoon, Raine saddled the pinto and rode down the little dirt road. She knew it would be better for her to stay home, but with her father due back later that night, she wanted at least to be able to mention Dek to him. The first question out of her father's mouth would probably concern Dek's spiritual relationship, and Raine needed some answers—as much for herself as for her father. How she would go about finding them out, she had no idea. Looping the reins around a branch, she walked up the porch steps and drew a breath for courage, then tapped on his door.

Dek's footsteps approached, and he opened the door. His brows rose, almost touching a wayward curl on his forehead.

"Raine."

"I . . . hope you don't mind. I was starting to talk to the walls."

"Not at all. Come in." He stepped aside to admit her. "Could I offer you some coffee or something?"

She shook her head. "Just your company. I promise I won't stay long. You're probably busy." She took the seat he indicated as he returned to his chair.

"Actually I was just sitting here staring at a book," he said, gesturing with his head toward a hardcover volume on the lamp table at his elbow. "I was about to pack it in anyway." He paused, studying her. "Been working on that drawing?"

"A little." Raine looked away. *I don't want to talk about art today,* she wanted to stay. *I want to talk about you. But how do I start?* Out of the corner of her eye she watched his long fingers absently stroke O'Clancy's rust-colored hair.

"So. Your father should be home later tonight, right? Where did you say he went?"

"To Edmonton. A religious retreat."

"Ah."

She knew from that nod of his that there was probably a smirk to go with it. She purposely avoided glancing his way for proof. "He enjoys that sort of thing, you know," she said defensively.

"I don't doubt it. And do you?"

Raine lifted her chin a fraction. "Awhile ago I might have said no. But that was because I was having a hard time dealing with some things."

"You mean the loss of your mother," he said on a kinder note. "That's always a rough one."

"Yes. Quite rough." She slowly met his eyes. "Are you speaking from experience? I . . . don't know anything about you, you know."

Dek smiled to himself. A fishing expedition, huh? She wanted information. Yesterday he would have bared his soul, but once he'd left her place the thawed spot had frozen over again inside. He wasn't so sure he wanted to heat it back up. "I've lost both my parents, so I do know how much it hurts. But like they say, time has a way of healing. Some things, anyway," he muttered almost as an afterthought. Getting up, he knelt before the hearth and stoked the softly crackling fire, then added another log.

"And sometimes faith helps a bit, too. In the hard times." Raine watched his back tense, and saw a muscle twitch in his jaw. She could feel him instantly pulling away, becoming remote as he rose and crossed the room.

Hands in his pockets, he remained with his back toward her as he idly turned the globe with one finger. "Well, at least you still have your father," he grated.

"True," Raine answered. *Isn't there still someone for you?*, she wanted so to ask. But seeing his slumped shoulders, she thought better of it.

"He probably doesn't even know his daughter consorts with a degenerate, does he?" Dek asked suddenly, swinging around. "Why do you, by the way?"

She felt her insides twist and knot under the heat of his glare. "I can't believe you said that. And I'll never believe you're a . . . degenerate. Not ever."

"Believe it. You should have ignored me from the first day you came across the creek. I'm not worth the time of day. For all you know I might even corrupt you—and how would your saintly father take that?" With a grimace he shifted his attention to the world outside the window.

A few heavy moments passed with nothing but the hiss of the new logs breaking the silence. Aware that she'd tapped into Dek's anger, Raine knew it was time for him to start bringing those deep feelings out into the open where they could begin to heal. Even if he decided to throw her out. "You know, I'd like my father to approve of my friends. Don't get me wrong. But I'm not a little girl. I do make choices of my own from time to time."

He turned, his expression hard. "Even when they might be detrimental?"

"They've never been so far," she said. "What is there about this one I'd regret?"

With a shake of his head, Dek shut his eyes for a second, then opened them.

"Why do you . . . close up whenever I mention something about faith, Dek?" she asked softly, watching as some unseen battle within him drew shutters tight, leaving his expression bland.

"Because I don't have any. And that's all you need to know."

Raine allowed her gaze to wander over his face, taking in the brittleness of his eyes, the grim line of his mouth. "I know how that feels, believe it or not. When we first moved to Canada my faith was in shambles. I blamed God for taking my mother away in her prime. I made up my mind never to speak to Him again. And I didn't, not for a long time."

Not hearing a response, she continued. "But feeling that way left me even more empty. Why do you suppose I pestered you so much?" She gave a little smile. "Perhaps you reminded me of myself! Someone who had no one to talk to, someone who could use a friend."

His shoulders shook with a silent huff.

"Oh, I knew you couldn't stand the sight of me at first," she went on. "I'm not dense. But the more you rejected me, the more determined I was to reach you, to help you. Funny thing was, I'm the one who was helped . . . more than you'll ever know."

"Yeah, well, that's great. But God took more than that away from me. A lot more. He took my—" his voice broke. He breathed in and out in shallow pants, like someone winded from a run, before he was able to go on. And when he spoke, the words came in near whispers, as though they'd never before been uttered aloud. "He took my career . . . and my wife. And left me with nothing."

Shocked, Raine felt her eyes water.

"Oh, but let's not forget these little beauties," he spat before she'd had a chance to answer, grasping a portion of his disfigured cheek cruelly between the thumb and finger of his equally scarred hand. "So wonder no more about my lack of faith. Now you can run along home to daddy and God and get on with your life." He gestured toward the door. "You know the way."

ten

Raine planted her feet and glared at Dek with her hands on her hips. "And what sort of friend would I be then, if I just walked away?"

Dek raked his fingers through his hair. Taking hold of her shoulders, he gripped firmly. "A former one. That's the only kind I need. Don't you understand? I'm used to being alone."

She tightened her mouth to keep back tears. "Well, sorry, but I'll never be a former friend or an ex-friend or any other yesterday kind of friend." She blinked, and a tear crested her lashes and spilled down her cheek. "You don't need to be alone. You should have someone around to talk to, like everyone else."

That tear was Dek's undoing. He never could stand to see a woman cry—or worse, make one cry. Now concerned more with her pain than his, he groaned. "Don't. Please. I'm really not worth it."

"Oh, yes you are, Alan Decker," she said with quiet conviction. "And I'll never give up until you can see that for yourself. I pray for you every day."

Dek pulled Raine close and held her against him, rocking her, unspeaking, inhaling the enticing perfume of her hair as his anger subsided and his pulse returned to normal. "You are without a doubt the most *stubborn* friend I've ever had. Do you know that?"

"Sorry," she said, lifting a watery smile. "I'll work on it."

"Guess that's as much as I can expect." He drew a long deep breath and slowly let it out. Easing her away, he held her at arm's length. "I can't promise I'll ever forgive God for what happened. That grudge is all that kept me alive for a few awful months. But who knows? Maybe in time I'll be able to at least come to terms with it."

"Then will you please stop trying to shut me out?" she asked.

He chuckled. No one had ever yet been able to stop the sun from shining. And though he didn't like to admit it, this young lady—missionary kid or not—had brought the first rays of sunlight into his life in years, illuminating all the remote corners of his being. Now, if given the choice, he wasn't all that certain he'd choose darkness ever again. "I promise."

Coming in after tending the horses the next morning, Raine hung her jacket and kicked off her boots, then met her father on his way to the kitchen. With a smile, she walked over for a hug. "I'm so glad you're home, Daddy."

"Me, too," he said, tightening the embrace before releasing her. "It's always good to get back."

"Well, you must be hungry. I was just about to make scrambled eggs. Want some?"

He nodded. Taking a mug from the cupboard, he filled it with coffee and took it to the table, where *The Red Deer Advocate* waited beside his plate.

"Looks kind of stormy out today," Raine said casually as she crumbled crisp bacon into the whipped eggs in the pan.

"Mm. The radio says it'll be unsettled for the next week. Might even get some more snow."

Raine glanced his way and saw that he had turned his attention back to the paper. She finished in silence. When everything was ready, she carried the plates in and took her seat. "Something wrong?" she asked, noticing his worried frown as he set the daily aside.

He smiled, and his expression softened. "It's all the unrest in Haiti. Can't help worrying a bit about Mark and the work there."

"I think about him a lot, too. Perhaps the clinic will have to close and the workers be sent to a safer place."

"Hope it doesn't come to that. It's so needed—especially with the unsettled political mess, the militant violence. As it is, medical facilities are far too inadequate. I can't see how they'd get by with any less." He paused. "Well, the whole thing's in the Lord's hands. We'll have to trust Him to look after Mark and Ruthie and everyone. I'd better say grace before our breakfast gets cold."

Raine bowed her head during her father's short prayer and afterward began eating. "So, you had a good time at Edmonton."

"Yes. I made quite a few interesting friends among the various groups, and we talked each other's ears off. Great fellowship. Can't say I didn't worry a little about you, though, on this big place by yourself."

Raine's throat tightened, and she almost couldn't swallow. Perhaps now would be a good time to tell her father about Dek. She took a sip of coffee and cleared her throat. "Daddy?"

He looked up, his blue eyes curious behind his glasses.

"I, um . . . wasn't by myself the whole time."

"You weren't?"

"No. I met someone a few weeks ago, and—"

"Oh, another young lady you can gossip with, huh? That's nice." He bit into his second piece of toast.

Raine suppressed a nervous laugh. Her insides were a quivering mass of jelly. Not a single one of the nice smooth speeches she'd been rehearsing would come to mind. "No, not a young lady. A man. A neighbor."

Her father's frown returned and deepened. "Oh. Do I know him from church or somewhere?"

She shook her head. "No. You haven't met him. He doesn't go to public places much."

Putting down his fork, her father just stared. "What sort of man wouldn't go out in public, pray tell?"

"Oh, Daddy, it's a long story. I met him soon after we moved here. I was down the lane sketching some different scenes, and I happened upon his place just across the creek."

"Funny you never mentioned him." Her dad pressed his mouth into a thin line.

"It just didn't seem important at the time. But our paths started crossing now and again, and—"

"And you started some sort of relationship or something?"

Raine hated the way that sounded, as though it were some sort of clandestine arrangement she should be ashamed of. "No," she answered.

"Well, obviously this stranger knew you enough to come by while I wasn't here."

Raine sighed. "Come on, Dad. I'm not a little girl anymore."

"Precisely." He folded his arms over his chest for emphasis.

The simple word did make her smile and gave her a needed boost of courage. "He's really very nice, you know. That day I got lost he found me and brought me home. He used to be an art professor, and I asked him for help with my drawing. He's been giving me lessons. We're friends."

"Friends," he echoed, shaking his graying head. "And you never once considered that I might like to meet this friend of yours? That's not like you."

"I know." Raine tried not to feel guilty. "I'm sorry. But I

really didn't mean anything by not telling you about Dek. Honestly."

"That's his name?" he asked. "Dek? This man who doesn't go out in public?"

Raine tipped her head slightly and met her father's eyes as she kept her voice strong and even. "His name is Alan Decker. The reason he keeps mostly to himself is because he's got some pretty bad scars. Until I came along, he had very little to do with folks in the area. I felt like I should reach out to him and be a friend. It's what you would do, and what the Lord would have done, I'm sure."

"Well," her father conceded, "hearing about him does shed a different light on the situation. Not that I'm entirely comfortable about it, you understand. You've been way too sheltered from the realities of the world. But I have every confidence that you'll be cautious in this—friendship. And you will also understand that I'd like to meet this man for myself."

"I'll tell him next time I see him." Raine breathed an inner sigh of relief. It hadn't gone as badly as she'd feared. And at least nothing came up about Dek's faith—or lack thereof. Yet.

Among the bustle at Calgary International Airport, Raine scanned the arriving passengers at Gate Six for Sarah's blonde head, then paced the waiting area during the interminable time it took for her to get through customs. At last the agent waved her through, and she stepped forth with her peaches-and-cream face beaming.

Raine grabbed her in a fierce hug. "Welcome to Canada! How was your trip?"

Sarah's laugh revealed even white teeth. "It seemed I was in the air forever. I quite began to wonder if I'd set foot upon solid ground again," she said, her musical British accent reviving treasured memories. She stepped back and tossed her head, her smooth chin length hair shining with the movement. "Oh, Raine, it's ever so good to see you again." Gray eyes sparkled beneath her long lashes.

Raine drank in Sarah's quiet elegance and smiled. Already it felt as though they had never been apart. "I thought today would never come."

"As did I," her friend agreed.

"Well, I'll be," said Raine's father, joining from the side-lines. "A familiar face at long last."

"Hello, Mr. Montrose," Sarah said, stepping into his open arms. "Awfully nice of you and Raine to meet me."

"Couldn't do anything but," he teased, releasing her. "Raine wasn't about to wait for you to make bus connections from here, you know. Good trip?"

"Splendid. The view of the mountains was breathtaking as we made our descent. The city looks huge from the air, and really quite lovely with its blanket of snow."

"It's nice here," he agreed. "But Rocky has a beauty of its own, too, as you'll soon see. We'd better claim your luggage, now. It's over this way."

Late afternoon waned as they finally arrived at Misty Hills. "Come on," Raine said. "I'll take you to your room so you can change into something comfortable. You'll get half the grand tour on the way, and the rest later. If you aren't too tired, that is." She led the way through the kitchen and living room and on to the bedroom wing.

"I am a bit tired," Sarah answered, a step behind, "but I'd love to see the rest of this charming place. Then we can stay up all night talking."

"What?" Raine's father injected with a chuckle, setting

Sarah's two suitcases on the big bed. "My ears are about to fall off from listening to you two talk nonstop for the last couple of hours. I'm ready for some aspirin."

The girls shared a laugh as they set a pair of small bags near the larger ones.

"Oh, Daddy, we have to make the most of what little time we have, you know."

"I suppose. Well, while you two visit I'll go see what I can rustle up for supper. How's that?"

"Great. Thanks." As her father left the room, Raine turned, smiling, and gestured with her arm. "Well, this is where you'll be staying, as you've probably guessed."

"Yes, quite," Sarah said, glancing about the arrangement of traditional furniture against the soft pastel wallpaper. "I must say, you've done a marvelous job on it. Lavender and violet, my favorite colors. Is yours near?"

"Just across the hall. I'm going to go put on some sweats while you change, okay?" At the doorway, she stopped and looked back. "By the way, I really love that gorgeous coat and traveling outfit."

Sarah raised her brows and brushed a graceful hand over her clothes. "Thanks. You know Auntie Maeve. Once she learned I was going to visit you, she sent me a wardrobe of everything in vogue. It was most unexpected, but nonetheless appreciated, of course."

Raine nodded slowly, watching Sarah unzip a suitcase. "She's sweet, and has such lovely taste. Well, I'll be back in a minute."

After supper, they hurried through the dishes and changed for bed.

"So, I've told you all the news from the clinic," Sarah yawned, clad now in brushed flannel pajamas and fuzzy slippers. She changed her position to cross-legged, hugging one of Raine's pillows against her slim form. "Now you must tell me about everyone I'll be meeting while I'm here. Starting with that Mr. Mysterious you told me about in your letters."

Raine averted her gaze and smiled. "He's really quite nice. His nickname is Dek."

"How did you meet? I believe you said it was accidental."

"Yes." A small twinge of discomfort sent color into Raine's cheeks. "I just happened to stumble upon his place. A little cabin in the woods, all off on its own."

"Hm." Sarah shrugged. "I can't imagine anyone wanting to live so cut off. From what I was able to see of this area on our way, it's mostly forest to begin with."

"But that's what he wanted—and for a good reason."

"What ever do you mean?" Sarah tilted her head.

"Some time ago he had some kind of accident and was severely burned." Raine watched her friend's eyes grow large at the statement, then continued. "One side of his face appears normal, perfect. You've no *idea* how perfect. At one time he must have been incredibly handsome."

"But now he's not?"

Raine gathered herself with a slow breath. "The other side is horribly scarred. His ear, his neck, possibly even his shoulder and arm, I can't be sure."

"How perfectly awful."

With a nod, Raine met Sarah's eyes. "I don't even know the full extent of the damage, really, and can't bring myself to ask. His left hand is quite disfigured, and I'm sure he must have once been left-handed. Often he goes to do something with that one first, then must switch to the other."

Frowning in sympathy, Sarah listened silently.

"He's terribly self-conscious about it—and I can understand the way he feels about his appearance. But, you know? I've been able to see past his scars all along. Right from the beginning he tried to repel my friendly overtures and keep me away. But something inside of me kept sending me back to try again."

Sarah nodded as a smile spread across her expressive lips. "Don't you find that somewhat curious?"

"What do you mean?"

"Well, we once made a solemn vow that after we left Haiti we'd never again aid another living soul. And now look at what you're doing!"

Raine giggled. "I meant to keep that oath, really. I was so weary of that life." With a shake of her head, her voice grew softer. "But I couldn't stop myself. I had to help him if I could." Glancing at her friend, Raine noticed that Sarah's blinks were lasting longer and longer as her eyelids grew heavy. She smiled to herself. "Hey, tomorrow's another day, right? I'd better let you sleep at least *one* night."

"Capital idea," she said with a yawn. "See you tomorrow, then." Getting up, Sarah walked quietly across the hall to her own room.

The next morning as Raine set out fresh water and feed for the horses, she heard footsteps. She looked up and met Sarah's bright smile as the girl approached in jeans and a hot pink parka. "Good morning."

"So it is." Looking from one animal to the other, Sarah moved first to Buckwheat and stroked the blaze on his chestnut face. "Look at this splendid lad. Hello, bonny boy," she crooned softly, and the horse nuzzled against her hand.

Raine smiled and reached for the hay fork, spreading fresh straw in the stalls. "I knew you'd like Buckwheat. He's so like your Brighton Prince."

"Yes." Looking around the roomy old barn, Sarah inhaled deeply. "I'd almost forgotten these honest, horsey smells. It's quite like being at Auntie Maeve's again. Will we be able to ride later, perhaps?"

"Sure. They'll be glad for the exercise. Let's go have some breakfast. and afterward we'll take these guys out."

Early that afternoon, they nudged their mounts out the ranch gate and turned down the lane. Sarah's face glowed from the crisp air. "It's truly magnificent," she breathed. "I can see why you've given those of us back in Haiti so little thought since your arrival."

Raine laughed lightly. "Little thought! I like that, when I missed you so much. But I have to admit it is nice here. I love it more every day."

"Does Dek know I'm coming?" Sarah asked.

"I didn't tell him the exact moment, but yes, he did know I've been expecting you. I told him I wanted him to meet you."

"I must confess I'm a bit nervous about it."

"Don't be," Raine said with a smile. "He's really nice. You'll like him, I'm sure."

Sarah craned her neck, taking in the vista surrounding them. The sunshine made snow-covered fields on either side glisten with pristine radiance. Through the bare tree branches, the western hills sparkled in the distance. Coming to the creek, the girls crossed the bridge and dismounted, securing the reins.

Raine glanced around with a frown. An odd apprehension filled her. Something was not quite right.

"What is it?" Sarah asked, studying her.

"I'm not sure." Raine motioned vaguely with a hand.

"There's no smoke from the chimney. And not so much as a footprint in the snow near the house—his or his dog's." She moved beyond the end of the porch and checked the barn. "Not even a horse track. Strange, it hasn't snowed for at least three days." Hurrying up the steps, she tried to control her uneven breathing as she knocked at the door. Once. Twice.

There was no answer.

eleven

Raine turned to Sarah in confusion. "Dek's not here—and apparently hasn't been for days. It doesn't make sense." Her shoulders sagged in disappointment as a pent-up breath released a puff of mist.

"Perhaps he's been called away. Some sort of family emergency," Sarah suggested in her practical way.

"He's never mentioned even having any family." Crossing to the window, Raine tried to peer inside the cabin, then gave up. She averted her attention to the overcast sky, which looked about as dismal as She felt. "Well, no point in hanging around. We'll have to come back another time." With a sigh, she shoved her mittened hands into her pockets and trudged down the steps.

They rode partway home in silence, the horses plodding along side by side.

"Raine?" Sarah asked.

Raine met her friend's inquisitive expression.

"I know this is prying, but just how much do you know about this chap?"

"What I've already told you. He's very private." Raine purposely hadn't told Sarah everything. The discomforting thought of Dek's having once been in love—and married—was taking time to digest, and she hadn't been able to bring herself to mention that. And now, this disappearance of his seemed like a deliberate snub—and it hurt.

Dek maneuvered the Bronco through the hairpin turns and switchbacks of the hilly Banff road and pulled into a familiar dirt drive, drawing to a stop at an attractive log cabin. Nestled in the spiky shade of lush evergreens and winter-bare aspen, the sight brought memories of nailing shingles and screening porches, projects which among others had helped him acquire much of his present carpentry skill. Getting out of the truck, he and Clancy went around back and bounded up the porch steps. Dek tapped on the storm door.

In moments footsteps approached. It swung open.

A huge, uncharacteristic smile spread across the crags of Carter Ross's long face. "Alan!" he boomed. "Aren't you a welcome sight!" Throwing wide the door, he gave Dek an enthusiastic hug, complete with thumps on his back.

"Carter," Dek grinned. "Hope you don't mind my dropping in out of the blue." Automatically, he used the bootjack to slip off his boots on the mat inside, then hung his jacket.

"Mind?" The elderly man shook his peach-fuzz head. "You're always welcome here. son, ya' know that. Come take a load off. But I don't mind sayin' ya look a mite peaked, though. Everythin' okay?" Bending and ruffling the dog's ears, he glanced up, his blue eyes curious.

Dek lifted his bandaged left hand with a wry grimace. "I sort of cut myself on a saw when I had something else on my mind."

"No!" Carter boomed. "Don't that beat all. Bad hurt?"

With a shake of his head, Dek grinned. "Naw. I needed to check in at the Center anyway. I'd been neglecting my hand exercises and started having problems, so I boarded Blackjack and drove out to Vancouver for a few days."

"Ah. The doctors got ya back on track now, have they?"

Dek nodded. "A slice here and there, a few stitches, a big lecture on the importance of using the muscles .... You name it, they dished it out."

Carter's mouth twitched, a gesture Dek had decided years ago was the man's alternative to smiling. But despite his usual dour expression, there was a constant twinkle in his small blue eyes. "Well, come sit a spell. Grace had to run a pup over to see the vet, but she'll be back any minute. Anyway, the coffee's always hot."

"So I remember." Dek followed his friend into the room papered in a cheery pattern of apples and fruit baskets, and sat at the table, resting his soft canvas cast beside the ever-present crocheted doily. The intricate design matched that of scarves, arm covers and head rests on the parlor chairs. Just outside the window, a few tentative snowflakes floated lazily in the frosty air. "Lucybelle have a new litter?"

"Yep," Carter answered, placing a steaming cup of coffee before Dek. He took a seat opposite. "Five pups, born—let's see—" Screwing up his grizzled face in one hand, he frowned in thought. " 'Bout seven weeks ago. Doin' fine, all but the runt. Take ya' out to see 'em in a spell. Lucybelle oughta be glad to see how her Clancy's grown so big." His mouth twitched as he scratched under the dog's chin.

Dek smiled and took a drink of the strong brew. "So how've you been?"

"Oh, the usual aches and pains. But thank the good Lord we get around pretty good, Grace an' me. How 'bout yerself?"

The sound of a car driving up eliminated the need to answer, and Carter rose. "Better go make sure she doesn't slip on the ice. Be right back."

In moments the door opened and closed, and a woman's plump face peeked in from the mud room, glowing from cold. A direct contrast to her serious-faced husband, Grace Ross looked as if she'd been born smiling and never stopped. Dek rose, and she beamed at him as she fumbled with coat buttons.

"Well, I declare. Alan. I couldn't believe it when I saw your truck in the drive." She unzipped her low, fur-cuffed boots, and replaced them with crocheted scuffies. Then, slipping off her wrap, she let her husband deal with it as she bustled inside. "Not a day goes by but we don't think about you and say a prayer for you."

"Hello, Grace." Dek opened his arms and strode to give her a hug. Her fine permed hair tickled his nose as he kissed the top of her head, then her cheek. "It's good to be back. I've missed you."

As they took seats, Carter came in with the pup and placed it in his wife's arms. "What'd the doc say?"

"Oh, says it's doin' okay." Cuddling the pup to her pillowy bosom, she nuzzled its reddish coat of fluff. "Fair to middlin' is the best we can hope for. We need to find her a home of her own pretty quick."

"Now," Carter admonished, "quit yer fussin'. She'll be okay, the doc said."

"I s'pose." Fine lines beside her eyes multiplied in number as she turned a smile on Dek and patted his forearm. "Sure is a treat to have you sittin' at the table again. How long's it been? Gonna stay awhile? You're skinny as a rake. Hungry? What happened to your hand? Tell us all about yourself."

Dek grinned and shifted in his chair.

Following the Sunday morning song service, Steven Grogan stepped to the pulpit for the pastoral prayer. Bright sunlight streaming through stained glass spilled a patch of blue over his sandy hair as he stood tall and straight in a navy wool suit.

Sarah leaned closer to Raine, eyes sparkling. "You only said he was handsome," she whispered. "He's devastating!"

Raine glared at her in mock seriousness, but her friend's persistent smile didn't diminish one iota as they bowed their heads. And the stubborn set of Sarah's jaw gave clear indication that a plan was already being formulated in her brain to draw the pastor's attention during her visit. Raine barely heard his prayer as she envisioned Sarah carrying out an infinite number of schemes.

"Our text this morning is the Ninety-first Psalm," the minister said. "A personal favorite of mine. I know many of you agree." With a smile, he opened his big Bible and began to read the chapter aloud.

After the conclusion of the service, Raine waited for the bulk of the congregation to leave before she finally led the way to the door, where the pastor stood shaking hands with the departing worshipers.

He looked at her with a smile and gave a warm handclasp. "Lorraine. Nice to see you this morning."

She returned the smile, then gestured beside her. "I brought someone to meet you. This is my friend, Sarah Hamilton. Sarah, this is Steven Grogan."

"Sarah?" Steve said, transferring his gaze to Raine's companion. "From the mission? I recognize you from the slides Lucas has." He took her hand.

"Quite right." Her cheeks pinkened as she lowered her lashes alluringly, then slowly raised them. "I've come for a short visit."

"Not too short, we hope. It's a pleasure to meet you. I expect you'll be attending regularly while you're here."

Sarah's smile rivaled the brilliance of the sun. "Why, yes, thank you. Rather lovely sermon, I must say."

"Excuse me," Raine finally said from the sidelines. "We'd be very happy to have you come to supper sometime this week, Steve, if you're free."

He flashed his most debonair smile. "Name the day," he said as his gaze made its way back toward Sarah and lingered.

Later that night, Sarah flopped across Raine's bed on her stomach, knees bent, fluffy lavender slippers dangling above her backside. She rested her chin in her cupped hands. "I can't believe I was such a flirt. At both services, no less. I'll never be able to hold up my head in public again."

Brushing her hair at the dressing table, Raine stopped mid-stroke and gave her friend a disbelieving look. "Oh, sure."

"No, really. You should've stopped me with a stout kick. For all I knew, you might have already staked him out for yourself, and I never so much as asked. And there I was, acting the perfect tart. Jolly well worse than a young girl just coming into blossom. Quite shocking."

Raine set down the brush and smiled at Sarah's humorous comment. "Oh, I'm sure he's used to unattached females who see him as fair game."

"Well? *Are* you interested?" She didn't appear to breathe as She waited for the answer.

Raine shrugged a shoulder. "Daddy would certainly approve, if I were."

"He's trying to arrange it?"

With a sigh, Raine crossed to the other side of the bed, where she sat on the corner. "Steve's been here to supper and taken me out once or twice. But, nice as he is, he reminds me so of Mark it's like dating my own brother."

"You know, there is a sort of resemblance, now that I think about it. But actually, I thought Mark rather dashing, too." Sarah giggled at Raine's look of shock. "Oh, come on. He is, you know." Then she turned serious. "I suppose your Dek What's-His-Name is the complete opposite, then."

"That's right." Raine didn't exactly feel like elaborating. Still trying to figure out what she considered his betrayal, she felt a burning in her eyes and blinked it away as she fidgeted with the satin bow on her nightgown.

Sarah broke the ensuing silence. "You might think I'm poking my nose where it doesn't belong, but . . ."

Raine tried to avoid Sarah's knowing gaze.

"You've never mentioned anything about his faith. Why ever not?"

Hoping to hide the flicker of guilt she felt inside, Raine attempted an expression of non-committal.

Sarah's eyes flashed, and she suddenly sat upright. "You know, old girl, after you went away I'd a lot of time to think about affairs of the heart. And I'm more certain than ever before that sharing that common bond is truly important—especially in any sort of lasting relationship."

With a sigh, Raine nodded slowly. "I know. I've always felt that way myself."

"Yet this friend of yours isn't a believer?"

Raine swallowed a lump in her throat. "I really can't be sure. He refuses even to mention God."

Taking one of Raine's hands, Sarah reached over and hugged her. "Then please be careful. Think it through before you get in too deep, okay? The 'unequal yoke,' and all that. You must be true to your own convictions. Never going back to Haiti, as we once vowed, is one thing, but allowing yourself to be pulled in another direction entirely . . . . We both dedicated our lives to God on the same night, remember? And He might have other plans for you."

"I remember." Tears welled in Raine's eyes as she stared at her hands.

"Here, have some more chicken and dumplin's," Grace ordered. "You need all you can get."

Dek grinned and shook his head. "Fatten me up too much, and I won't fit into my jeans tomorrow."

"Yeah, quit yer fussin'," Carter added. "Leave the boy alone."

"Well, he's nothin' but skin and bones," she said, "like when we first took him in all those years ago so he wouldn't freeze to death." Her expression softened under Dek's amused one. She sighed heavily. "Oh, don't pay me any mind. I'm just so glad to see you."

"That goes for me, too," Carter said. "Been a long time since ya hiked across country as a young lad. I feel proud every time I think of how ya worked your way through art school. Sure come a long way since then."

Rising, Grace cleared away the plates and serving bowl, replacing them with a homemade apple pie. Then, after taking her seat, she quartered the pastry, putting three pieces on dessert plates. She passed one to Dek.

He rolled his eyes and grinned at her, then forked a slice into his mouth.

She gave him a conspiratorial smile. "Good to see some of those hard lines in your face startin' to disappear, like you're comin' back to life again. Gonna tell us about her?"

Dek swallowed too fast. "Huh?" he managed finally, aware of a warm glow spreading upward over the normal side of his face, turning his ear scarlet.

Grace shot a sideways glance at her husband. "See?"

His mouth twitching as he watched the exchange between the other two, Carter broke into a hearty laugh. "Come on, old woman. He'll tell us when he's good an' ready. Let's finish dessert, so we can have our evenin' devotions." Reaching out toward the buffet on his left, he removed a book containing scripture selections for every day of the year and set it beside Dek. "You can do the honors when you're done."

Dek lowered his gaze to the worn book. Obviously, it still meant as much to them now as it had when he'd bought it for them as a lad of seventeen. But could its words still speak to him, much less have any credibility? He gave fleeting thought to asking for another slice of pie, anything to delay the inevitable. But he already felt close to bursting, and not for anything in the world would he hurt two of the dearest people in his world. He steeled himself and opened to the proper date, then began reading the evening selection:

> *I have loved you with an everlasting love; therefore I have drawn you with lovingkindness.*
>
> *Like an eagle that stirs up its nest, that hovers over its young, He spread His wings and caught them, He carried them on His pinions. He lifted them and carried them all the days of old.*
>
> *Behold, I have refined you, but not as silver; I have tested you in the furnace of affliction—*

Dek felt the kitchen closing in on him and couldn't breathe. Perspiration trickled down his spine. He rose, pushing his chair back with his legs. "Sorry. Excuse me." Without further explanation, he shoved the book Carter's way and fled in haste down the basement steps, to the room which once had been his and even yet sported trophies and ribbons he'd won while attending university. Sinking onto the twin bed which was less than adequate to fit the length of his frame anymore, he rested his head on his bent arm and stared at the ceiling.

His *refinement* had come with a high price tag. Fragments

of that horrific night would forever pierce his memory: Driving home from the art exhibit with the windows open; a distant explosion; rounding the last bend and seeing the house engulfed in flames. Then a slow-motion sequence of events. Annie! Kicking in the door. Smoke. Faint sirens. Something striking his head, and his hand flying up in reflex as a portion of the ceiling crashed down on him. Why had the firemen dragged only *him* out? A loving God would have spared Annie. She was so good. So special. He ground his teeth.

Moments passed before he became aware that not a sound carried from upstairs. He wondered what Carter and Grace must have thought of his flight. They'd been through nearly the whole ordeal with him, and though he'd never voiced his bitterness aloud in their presence, neither had he found comfort in the prayers they had whispered at his side, or in their scriptural platitudes. They must have known he was angry at God. And still was.

O'Clancy set his rump down on the braided oval rug and rested his head on Dek's chest with a whine.

He ignored the animal.

Dek stepped outside into the pure, translucent light of day. He'd forgotten his shoes, and was in his shirt sleeves, but he felt no winter chill. All around him, everything glowed fresh and green, the effervescent green of spring. Blooming in profusion, flowers in myriad colors dripped over fences, entwined slender tree trunks, grew in clusters, capped hills. A splashing sound came from a few yards away, where a waterfall spilled in crystal glory gently down a rock precipice. Birds of indefinable varieties flitted and darted in joyous flight. One, an incredible blue, lit on a branch near Dek's shoulder and broke into song. He held his breath so it wouldn't fly off.

"Over here," came a woman's voice, familiar and light. He focused his gaze in the direction of its source. "Over here," she said again. "Find me."

He filled his lungs, and the bluebird fluttered away silently, on wings fragile and lacy as those of a butterfly. Distant music, faint yet coming from all around, filled the air.

"This way," said the voice, and a lilting laugh came to him on the mild breeze.

Frowning in wonder, Dek slowly made his way over ground cushiony and cloudlike beneath his feet. Rounding a tree, he caught the briefest glimpse of a slender form in white. She darted out of sight.

"Annie?" he called incredulously.

Laughing she peeked from behind a boulder and stepped out.

"Annie!"

"I wondered if you would come, my love." She drew nearer, her gossamer gown whispering around her slim ankles.

Dek stared, afraid to believe she was real. How could she be there? His gaze drank in the sight of her. Her dark, silken hair had grown nearly to her waist and now glistened beneath a coronet of white flowers. "I thought—"

"I can stay only a moment," she said, slipping her tiny hand inside his.

He lifted it to brush her fingers with his mouth. His breath caught. It had no scars. He felt his face, and it, too, was whole. He had no words to speak. "Come home with me," he finally managed.

"I cannot. I am needed here. I help care for the babies . . . there are so many little babies."

He could not stop looking at her angel-innocence, the beautiful glow on her face. He reached to touch it, to stroke *her rose-petal skin, and felt his eyes grow moist.*

"You are so sad," she whispered. "You must not be sad over me. I am very happy. But I must go now, and so must you . . . . Someone needs you." She placed a white rose in his left hand, then on tiptoe, gave his cheek a sweet kiss. "My prayers are with you."

"But—"

"Will I ever . . . see you again?"

Though barely audible, her question pierced his soul. "Yes," he tried to say, clutching the rose tightly. No words came. He tried again, louder. "Yes. I promise."

The harsh sound of his voice jolted him. Heart pounding, Dek opened his eyes. The room was shrouded in darkness, except for the yard light outside. Slanting through the pleated curtain on the small basement window, it cast oblique shadows here and there. How long had he been asleep?

He sat up and rubbed his eyes. His cheeks were damp. The hand in the cast throbbed as he struggled to recall the dream to his memory. But already the colors and fragrances and sounds were fading, like watercolors blurring into a single indistinct hue. He released a sigh. At least his beautiful Annie was safe. Happy. He let the peace of that thought pour over his jagged nerves like a healing balm.

Then another statement impressed itself upon his consciousness. She said she was praying for him! His mouth curved into a grim smile, and he shook his head. No matter how hard he tried to shut God out of his life, no matter how far he'd run, everyone he knew seemed to be praying for him. Unbelievable. How like her to have told him that. He felt the smile vanish as her sweet voice echoed again in his heart.

Will I ever see you again?

Dek hoped so. He emptied his lungs. Who knows . . . maybe

there was something in that prayer stuff after all. Even for him.

He thought back over his life. At home back in Toronto, there had been no love after his mother had passed on. She had been all he had in his life. She had worked herself to death trying to make a home for them after his father had walked out with someone half her age. They had never heard from him again. When his mom had died, Dek had nowhere to go. He packed a bag and hitchhiked west.

Not until Carter and Grace Ross had crossed his path and taken a liking to him had Dek ever known a sense of family, of belonging. Of faith. After observing the selfless example of two people who lived what they believed day by day, Dek finally acknowledged his own need of salvation and accepted Jesus as his Savior. It was the first time in his life he found peace. That had lasted until the night of the fire. In its aftermath, he bitterly turned his back on God and all things related.

Now, suddenly, it seemed everyone he knew was praying for him. Dek could feel the pull of those prayers as they gained ground, drawing him back. He had been running forever, and now felt the Lord's gentle hand on his shoulder, fastening him to the here and now. What was the use of trying to hide any longer? He was weary of it. There was only one way to find the peace he used to know.

Sinking down to his knees, Dek bowed his head in prayer.

twelve

Raine fluffed her pillow for the tenth time, then lay back down on her side. The clock face on the nightstand glowed three a.m. Soon the relentless pale blush of morning would steal over the darkness outside, and it would be time to get up. Hoping a glass of milk would help make her sleepy, she flung the covers aside and reached for her robe and slippers, then padded silently to the kitchen.

The refrigerator light illuminated the remainder of the fudge marble cake Sarah had baked to impress Steve when he'd come for supper. It had worked, too, Raine recalled with a wry smile. Men were such pushovers. Taking out the dessert, she cut herself a slice and carried it to the table with a glass of milk, sitting at her usual spot in the dim room.

As she ate, she could still envision Sarah across the table, elegant in a silver, crushed-silk dress that matched her eyes. Steven had been impressed by more than a mere cake. Even before the meal had ended, he and Sarah had overcome their initial nervousness and relaxed in one another's company. They shared a number of common interests and had spoken easily of past experiences and present hopes. Remnants of their conversation still seemed to hover in the air, as if Raine could reach out and pluck a phrase from this sentence or that. Once again she had noticed Steve's way of looking at everything from the spiritual side. Sarah's comments had blended right in.

Raine lifted her glass and drained it, then took the dishes to the sink and returned to her bedroom. She was happy for Sarah. If her friend's attraction to Steven Grogan ended up to be mutual—and even turned into something lasting—great. They could do far worse than choose each other, though what Sarah's family would think if their only daughter decided to stay on in Canada remained to be seen. Anyway, Raine reminded herself, she had a serious problem of her own.

Thoughts of Dek crowded all others aside. A smile tugged at Raine's lips at the remembrance of their times together, of his helping her up after she'd tripped, of his spontaneous hug. It had felt so good to be in his arms. More than good. It felt right, somehow. She loved the sound of his voice, the twinkle in the depths of his eyes, his wit. Yet there was something more to consider. She couldn't help but compare her relationship with Dek to Steve and Sarah's—whose fellowship would not only span time, but would continue on through all eternity as well. Could there ever be that sort of harmony and oneness between herself and Dek? Between Dek and her father? Sarah's admonition still echoed in Raine's mind. "Be careful," she had said. "The unequal yoke, and all that."

A dull ache crept into Raine's heart. She hadn't needed a reminder of the night they both had decided to dedicate their lives to God. Her own devotional readings had kept the memory ever constant. The commitment had not been made lightly or on the spur of the moment, and despite the exquisite temptation which faced her in her attraction to Dek, she would never ask to take back her vow. Her life belonged to the Lord. All of it. And she had no right to pursue a relationship with a man who had no use whatsoever for God.

Without even trying to hold back her welling tears, she got out of bed and knelt beside it. "Dear Heavenly Father," she sobbed, then knowing it was useless to try speaking over the tightness in her throat, she continued silently. *Forgive me for being disobedient. I know I've created this problem for myself*

*by walking boldly into the lion's mouth instead of fleeing from
temptation. I don't know why I've felt so drawn to Alan
Decker. At first I thought I could help him. But now I see
that his problems are way too deep. I know nothing is
hidden from You, not even the fact that I'm in love with him,
So if I must live forever without him, please give me the
strength to do it. I never want the love I feel for him to be
stronger than that which I have for You. I want to be faithful
always, Father. And I will do what I must. She paused and
drew a deep breath. Help me to tell Dek . . . goodbye.*

Crawling back into bed, Raine cried herself to sleep.

"Isn't this the most magnificent day ever?" Sarah sighed,
crunching into her toast the following morning. "I just know
every part of it will be grand."

Raine eyed her silently, trying to ignore the headache that
tightened cords of iron around her temples. How could it be
morning already? She'd had trouble just putting one foot in
front of the other to get up and make breakfast.

"Well," came her father's reply, "looks like one of us must
have special plans."

Sarah blushed. "I've been invited to accompany Steve on
hospital visitation in Red Deer." She switched her attention
to Raine. "And you're more than welcome to come along, if
you like."

Raine smiled weakly. "Thanks, but no. I really don't care
to. You two go."

"But, hon," her father began, leveling clear blue eyes her
way as he lay his newspaper aside. "It might do you some
good to get out of the house for awhile, see something besides
these four walls."

His feeble attempt to push her and Steve together despite

any enthusiasm on her part irritated her all the more. "I'm really not up to it, Daddy. I have a headache. But," she said, glancing at Sarah, "I appreciate the offer. Steve's really good company. Enjoy yourself."

Her friend brightened visibly. "I'm sure I will. But I am sorry you're not feeling well. Anything I can do?"

With a shake of her head, Raine smiled. "I'll be fine. Soon as I finish my tea and see to the animals, I'll go lie down for awhile."

"Don't be silly," her father said, standing. "*I'll* make sure the horses get fed. You go and take some aspirin." Walking to the door, he took his coat and went out.

"Sure you won't change your mind?" Sarah asked. "A bit of fresh air might help, you know."

Raine patted her hand. "Couldn't you just see me along on your date? Miss Fifth Wheel?"

Sarah giggled. "Well, if you're that sure. He's awfully dashing. I'm rather looking forward to spending the day with him. Do you think this outfit will do?" She got up and twirled once, fanning out the pleated navy and cranberry plaid skirt beneath the coordinating sweater. Creamy pearls, gracing her neck and earlobes, caught and reflected the light with her movements, as did the gold barrette pinning back one side of her shining blonde hair.

Raine assessed her friend's lustrous eyes and daintily flushed cheeks, realizing suddenly that Sarah had grown quite lovely since the days when they had attended nursing school and ogled the professors. "Don't worry. He'll approve."

That afternoon a soft wind stirred the tree branches outside Raine's bedroom window, ruffling the needled boughs. She'd lain watching the swaying movement for some time and rose to have a better look.

An arc of high clouds crested the western sky. Curious, she raised the window a few inches. The breeze felt incredibly warm. Already the accumulated snow on the barn roof had begun to melt. Water dripped from the shingles and formed puddles on the ground. Dek had spoken of just such a phenomenon that day at the stonewall, calling it a chinook. She'd thought at the time that he was joking, but this was certainly worth checking out. She dressed hurriedly.

Outside, perched atop the main gate, Raine loosened her scarf and unzipped her jacket partway, breathing deeply of the balmy air. Incredible, she thought. Only hours before, the temperature had been near freezing, and now it felt like December had somehow turned into April. She wasn't about to let a minute of this reprieve from winter—however temporary—go to waste. Her headache had begun to ease noticeably as soon as she'd stepped out into the mild weather, and she figured a little walk might make it go away entirely. Jumping down, she put her hands in her pockets and stepped onto the lane.

Reaching the edge of the southern boundary of Misty Hills, Raine climbed up on the stonewall and stretched out her legs, filling her lungs with the smell and feel of the promise of spring. Nice as it was, going back to winter after this would be a drag.

On the logging road above the ranch, a pickup from a neighboring farm roared by. After it was gone, not another sound broke the stillness.

Raine glanced down the lane. Dek's place wasn't too much farther. She didn't especially want to *see* him, and even if she did, she certainly wasn't planning to confront him about skipping out. A tiny voice inside cautioned that she should not go at all. But a little part of her needed to know if he had returned. One quick peek would do.

She saw him in the distance in the corral, brushing Blackjack's winter coat with long smooth strokes. His back was to her, so she took a leisurely look as she moved a step closer. A twig snapped under her foot. She froze.

O'Clancy perked up from his position near Dek and sniffed the air.

Raine watched with a sinking feeling as the dog gave a joyous bark and jumped between the rails, heading right for her.

Dek set down the grooming brush and leaned an elbow on the fence as Raine stooped and gave the setter a hug. He waved when she glanced up.

With a polite answering flick of the hand, Raine turned and started back toward home, calling herself every stupid name she could remember.

"Raine," he yelled.

Only hesitating for a split second, she continued on.

"Raine! Wait, would you?"

She could barely hear Dek over the pounding of her heart. What on earth had she been thinking? Last night she'd made up her mind that when—and if—she ever saw him again, it would be only to say goodbye. Nothing else. Not discounting her renewed vow to the Lord, the feeling that Dek had deliberately snubbed her still carried a twinge of hurt. She'd really only wanted to assure herself that he was home again. She had not intended to come so close, but Clancy had spoiled everything. And now as she watched the dog take off after a rabbit, she didn't even have *him* to hide behind anymore. Trying to calm herself, she took a steadying breath as Dek strode near.

"Hi," he said.

She gave a nod without meeting his eyes.

"So, what do you think of the chinook?" He tipped his head, peering steadily at her.

She shifted uncomfortably to her other leg. "It's nice," she said, her voice a touch too high to sound casual as she'd intended. "Thought I'd take a walk and enjoy it."

"Ah. Something wrong?"

"What could be wrong?" Raine curled her fingers so tightly into her palms that they hurt as she struggled to keep her temper in check. Nearly as angry with herself as she was with him, she felt two hot spots of color high on her cheeks, and kept her eyelids lowered. If there was anything she couldn't afford to do, it was look into those compelling brown eyes of his.

"Could I offer you some coffee?"

"No, thanks. I have to get home."

"Why? You just got here."

So did you, she wanted to shout, but clamped her teeth together. Looking everywhere but at his face, her vision stumbled upon his cast, and her heart stopped. It was all she could do not to reach out and touch it. Her glance shot up to him. "What happened?"

"I was stupid. It's nothing major." He grinned. "It's all taken care of. They released me."

"That's where you've been?" she whispered, then blushed and looked away. "I mean. . . ."

Dek smiled and brushed a wayward curl from her eyes with his finger. Behind her long lashes, her green eyes swam in shimmery moisture. "What did you think?" he asked gently. "That I'd deserted you?"

"Something like that." She jutted out her chin and swallowed. "I'm sorry. It isn't like you owe me any explanations or anything." She paused, looking once more at his hand, then up again. "Are you really okay?"

"Yeah. Really." He studied her. "Hey, I . . . brought you something."

"You did?"

He nodded. "Inside. Sure you wouldn't like some coffee?"

She hesitated an instant, then moistened her lips, aware she was about to make the biggest mistake of her life. "Have any hot chocolate?"

He gave a hearty laugh. "You bet." Putting an arm around her shoulder, he turned with her and walked toward the house.

Raine slid her own arm around his waist. Even if she'd regret it later, surely she deserved at least this much. It might be all she could ever have. She barely let herself breathe, for fear she'd awaken from a dream. She inched her lashes upward and met his smile.

"Sure hope you like it," he said as they mounted the porch steps. He released her and opened the door.

Expectantly she stepped inside, wondering what Dek could possibly have chosen for her. They removed their jackets, and he took them both, tossing them on a chair. She let herself drink in the muscled shoulders and strong back beneath the charcoal wool sweater and checked shirt he wore.

"Wait here." Steering her to the couch, Dek left the room and returned within moments with a small squirmy bundle. Barely maintaining a straight face, he placed it on her lap.

An Irish setter puppy wriggled out of the blanket.

"Ohh, Dek," Raine gasped, gathering the warm softness and nuzzling it against her face. "How beautiful." She curled her arms around the puppy and stroked its soft coat of copper fuzz as she smiled at Dek.

He exhaled audibly with relief. "Like her?"

"Oh, yes. I've never had a dog of my own."

"Well, you have now. She's Clancy's little sis. You'll need somebody to keep a watchful eye when you're out sketching next summer, you know. And," he said, motioning toward the lamp table. "I even got you a book to help out."

"I—I can't believe this," she said, laughing softly. "If I didn't have my hands full right now, I'd—" overwhelming surprise made her more bold than cautious "—kiss you."

A slow smile spread across his mouth. "Hey," he said, his voice low, teasing. "No problem."

In an incredibly smooth succession of motions, Dek nudged the pup off her lap and drew her up into his arms. Ever so slowly, ever so gently, he covered her lips with his.

Raine couldn't believe this was happening. Not to her. Not now. Weak-kneed, she melted against him, lost for a moment in the wonder of his kiss, all too aware of the way her heart thundered against his as she threaded her fingers into his rich, curly hair. She wanted the moment to go on forever.

Any doubts she'd had before coming here evaporated with his touch. She would never love anyone in the world the way she loved Alan Decker.

It would make saying goodbye to him ten thousand times harder. But she had a promise to keep.

A tear escaped from the corner of her lashes.

thirteen

When at last the kiss ended, Raine rested her cheek against Dek's solid chest for a moment as he held her tenderly, stroking her hair. She felt his warmth seep into her and wanted to stay there forever, drinking in the strength of him, the scent of soap and musk and outdoors. Easing back slightly, she saw that his brown eyes mirrored all of her own longings. Sweet. Precious. Forbidden.

"Raine, I—"

His voice brought her back to reality. "No," she countered, touching her fingertips lightly to his mouth. "Don't say it. Please." Gathering whatever remnants of strength she could find, she let her hands fall rigid to her sides and drew away.

Dek lowered his arms in puzzlement. "You want me to lie to you?"

"No. I don't want you to say anything." Aware of the flush spreading over her face—and the pained shock on his—Raine averted her gaze. Catching sight of her jacket on the chair across the room, she bolted to it and tugged it on.

Only a step behind, Dek took hold of her elbow and turned her around. "Hey, look," he said. "If it's an apology you want—"

Raine shook her head. She was unable to meet his eyes through her blur of tears and knew she couldn't afford to look at him again anyway—not if she wanted to make this break quick, clean. By force of will, she steeled herself against the anguish in his voice and spoke evenly. "This whole thing was my fault. I had no right to come here today. Or ever, for that matter."

"What?" His face went ashen.

"I . . . won't be coming back. I'm sorry." She stumbled for the door. Grabbing the knob, she wrenched it open and fled.

Dek felt his mouth gape. A barrage of emotions surged through him in a split second, each one at war with the next. She couldn't really be leaving. Not like this. "Hey," he called inanely as the puppy tripped over his boot. "Aren't you forgetting something?"

She didn't look back. Didn't answer.

Completely confused, Dek whacked the door with his palm, and it slammed shut. He raked his fingers through his hair. What had just happened? One shining moment Raine had been fragile and trembling in his embrace, responding to his kiss in a way which spoke of belonging, of dreams, and the next, she'd spouted a farewell speech and vanished. Even as he replayed the entire scene in his mind he was at a loss for an explanation. Except maybe one.

A sliver of moon gleamed in the clear, starry sky as Steven's car pulled into the drive and stopped.

"I shall never forget this day," Sarah said as he walked her to the door. Unsure of herself, she turned in the circle of the porch light and extended her hand. "I had a lovely time."

Steven smiled. Taking her proffered hand, he raised it to his mouth and kissed it lightly. He locked his gaze on hers. With her fingers still curled within his, he drew her, unresisting, to himself. "I've no idea how I managed to keep from doing this until now," he murmured.

Sarah closed her eyes momentarily in the hollow of his shoulder. "I'm glad you finally relented," she whispered. Then, shocked, she blushed. "I can't believe I just said that."

"Why not? Didn't you mean it?" Steve asked, drawing

back with a playful grin.

"Yes, of course. But I wouldn't want you to think—"

"Ah, Sarah," he said, taking her face in his hands. He traced her cheekbones with his thumbs as his smoldering gaze quietly devoured her. "If you knew what I was thinking right now, you'd know you have nothing to fear. And to prove that, I'll even let you go in. Right after this." Touching his mouth lightly to hers, he kissed her. " 'Night."

"Goodnight," she whispered. Stepping inside, she closed the door, but watched through the windowpane until he drove off. After the lights of his car disappeared from view and her heartbeat returned to a more sedate pace, she floated up the steps and into the kitchen.

The house lay in stillness, lit by a dim lamp. Biting back disappointment over having to wait until morning to tell Raine about her date, Sarah draped her coat over a chair back, then flicked the light off and tiptoed toward the guest room.

As she reached her door, she thought she heard a muffled sound coming from across the hall. She stopped and listened until it came again.

Crying.

Her heart contracted. Hesitating only a second, she moved to the door and opened it silently.

In the glow filtering through the sheer priscillas, she could make out Raine weeping into her pillow. "Raine? It's Sarah," she whispered, entering the room. "Are you all right?"

Raine choked on a sob. Clenching the pillowcase tightly in her fists, she finally raised her head, then buried it again.

"It might help to talk."

Slowly sitting up, Raine drew her knees to her chin and tried uselessly to wipe her wet cheeks with her fingers. "Oh, Sarah," she moaned. "I wish I were dead." Taking out a fresh tissue, she blew her puffy nose.

Sarah sat beside Raine and lifted an arm, and Raine swayed against her. With her other hand, Sarah brushed damp hair away from her friend's swollen eyes. "Now why ever would you say that? Tell Auntie all about it."

The simple childish phrase they had used whenever either of them had a problem brought a tiny smile, but it flickered and wilted instantly. Raine sniffed, and another tear dropped onto her nightie.

"Has this anything to do with Dek?" Sarah asked.

Raine nodded.

"You've seen him, then?"

Another nod.

"Well, what is it? Has he done something to hurt you?"

Raine shook her head and winced. "It's worse than that," she said, feeling her throat muscles clench again. She swallowed. "I . . . I . . . hurt *him*." At that her voice broke on a new rush of sobs. She flung the worthless tissue to the floor, where it joined others.

"There's a good girl," Sarah said, giving a little hug. "Cry it all out."

Raine struggled to breathe. Her head ached. Her heart ached. She hurt all over. Her body burned with the memory of Dek's embrace and her response to his kiss. Where she'd ever found strength enough to leave, she had no idea. When finally her crying subsided, she sniffed and pulled out another tissue from the nearly empty box. "I must look a fright," she said, combing fingers through her bedraggled hair.

Sarah smiled gently.

Feeling a cramp in the pit of her stomach, Raine hunched forward. "It's all my fault. All of it."

"What is?"

"The whole thing. I knew better than to get involved with him."

"It's that bad, then?"

"Pretty much." Raine made a helpless gesture, laughing and crying at once. "I *thought* I was going to help him. The poor, lonely exile. I wanted to be his friend, show him that he's still a person of worth even if he does have some scars."

"Only it got a bit out of control. And friendship wasn't quite enough."

Raine nodded sadly. "It was at first." She balled the tissue in her fingers, absently shredding it with her nails as she spoke. "Funny, I was so stupid I didn't realize that he wasn't the only lonely one, I started baking things for him. Started going down there all the time—to have art lessons . . . or so I told myself."

"Hm. How about Mr. Decker?" Sarah asked. "Did he seem to accept that?"

Raine slanted a glance at her. "I really don't know. In the beginning he thought I was just a pest, something he'd put up with until I finally went away. But you know me. It made me all the more determined to show him I was somebody who cared."

"And he started to understand," Sarah probed.

Lowering her attention to her hands, Raine let out a weary sigh. "Oh, he understood, all right. Tonight he . . . almost said he . . . loved me." She blotted the corners of her eyes and continued. "He'd brought me a beautiful little puppy—can you believe it? I was so surprised . . . . And just last night I renewed my vow to God. I told Him I'd say goodbye to Dek." Turning away, she felt hot tears as a new onslaught of sobs shook her.

"Ah," Sarah said when she quieted. "You kept the promise, then?"

Recapturing a measure of composure, Raine nodded. "Hardest thing I've ever done in my life. It would have been easier to cut out my own heart." She paused for a few seconds. "I didn't even take the puppy. I really hurt him. I can't believe I was so dumb. I feel so rotten."

"Did you tell him the reason for your leaving?"

"How could I?" Raine asked glumly. "It would only have made matters worse, learning he was in a competition with God and came in second. He'd never have been able to understand that."

With a tiny smile, Sarah patted Raine's knee. "Well, this is small comfort, but I'm sure you made a wise decision."

"I only hope you're right." Raine shook her head sadly. "Pray for him, Sarah, okay? I know he's hurting right now. I really made a mess of things."

"I'll pray for both of you," her friend answered. Rising, she gave Raine's hand a squeeze. "Things might look a bit bleak at the moment. but they usually have a way of working out . . . eventually."

"Hmph." Raine smirked. "If we live so long. Only somehow, I can't see this particular problem ever being resolved. "

Sarah gave an understanding nod. "But then, that's what faith's all about, isn't it?" Bending over, she gave Raine a kiss on the cheek, then straightened.

Raine watched Sarah cross to the door. "Thanks for listening," she whispered. Then with a sigh, she sank back down on her pillow.

The dark night had long since spread its black cloak over the earth before Dek even undressed. The painful throbbing in his damaged hand had gradually eased, becoming an itch in the healing process. Absently he rubbed the fresh bandage.

His jaw muscles ached from having been clenched for the last half of the day, and he forced them to relax as he pulled on his pajama bottoms. His cheek burned and twitched from not wearing his scarf over the vulnerable scars that afternoon. Automatically he reached for the medicated lotion from the burn center and carefully applied some to his face and neck, noticing in the mirror that the hue of the thick scars had deepened from the usual rose to an angry maroon.

His eyes traced the waxy disfigurement down his neck and over his marbled shoulder, down his puckered, hairless arm. He looked with contempt at his left hand, remembering the weeks it had been a bandaged club, oozing and putrid. Exercise had coaxed it from the crusted claw shape it had curled into when his once long fingers looked like decayed leather, like old leaves whose rich color had been sucked away by a cold winter. Never again would they possess their former strength or skill. It had been a challenge to learn to be right-handed. Turning a fraction, he assessed with scorn the donor sites on his scarred back, where long strips of healthy skin had been peeled away, leaving outlines of pale anemic patches among the rest of the unmarred flesh.

A real prize, he was. He might as well face it. He barely resembled the photographs Grace Ross kept on her mantel from when he was athletic and muscular. When he was normal. Gritting his teeth, he pulled on his flannel top, even yet begrudging the fact that his scars needed to be shielded from temperature changes and always would.

A rush of bitterness flooded his veins, gaining strength with each throb of his heart. What gall he must have possessed to think he could ever be anything to Raine but a friend. She had been repulsed when he kissed her.

He shot a glance back at his image in the mirror, at the

grotesque mutant who reflected back at him. Blindly, Dek turned and hurled the medication across the room, deriving perverse satisfaction as it shattered and spilled down the wall and onto the carpet. Then he flung a towel after it and shook his head as he sunk down onto his bed. Hunched over, he put his head in his hands and drew a tortured breath.

He wanted to hate Raine Montrose. Mere weeks ago he would have curled his lip in grim satisfaction if she'd finally gone back where she belonged. Out of his life. He didn't need her.

But he couldn't get past the vision of shimmery green eyes, red-gold hair, and sweet smiles that had engraved themselves upon his brain. Every time he closed his eyes she was there to haunt him, awakening a hunger for rekindled faith, reminding him of how pathetic his life had been before she'd moved to the farm up the lane. She had splashed subtle rainbows across endless, colorless days, breaking down all the walls he'd so carefully constructed around his haven. Little by little the last of his flimsy defenses had finally crumbled, and he'd grown to love her. No longer attempting to fight it, he let the realization unfold in his mind like the petals of a flower in the morning sun.

Clancy's deep snore rumbled from the other side of the room. In a box beside the bed, the pup whimpered and snorted in sleep.

The combination of sounds caused a hollow ache in Dek's gut, and he cringed at an unwelcome memory.

"I won't be coming back." She might as well have shouted the words for the way they lanced his heart, draining the last drop of blood from his being. As long as he lived they would echo over and over in the dark recesses of the night, ricocheting off a chasm inside that he'd never known existed until she came along. He felt sick to his stomach.

Raine wasn't to blame. But the profound emptiness she'd left behind would be a long time going away.

fourteen

A stiff north wind brought a sudden unexpected end to the mild chinook. Dek lay awake for much of the night listening to its howling as it rattled shutters and whistled through trees. After he had finally dozed off, an unusual stillness woke him. With a grimace he dragged himself out of bed and yanked the nylon cord which opened his curtains.

The sight that met his eyes stole his breath away. Hoar frost had turned the surrounding landscape into a sparkling fairytale, painting every branch and wire with fragile crystals of white. Raine would be awed by the incredible spectacle, he was sure. He could just imagine the glow in those sea green eyes of hers.

Then remembrance of yesterday brought a hollow ache. Raine was gone. He'd never know what she thought about anything ever again. Dek's own joy over nature's beauty dulled. Turning away from the window, he grabbed his jeans from the chair and dressed woodenly. He'd get over it. He'd gotten along fine before she came along, and he'd survive this loss as well.

"Come on, Clance," he said, bending to stroke the dog's ears. "You too, pup." Straightening, he strode from the room and went to the kitchen, where he shooed the animals out the back door. After starting some coffee, he poured dog food and puppy chow into two bowls. He hadn't planned on having two dogs to care for. Besides, he was running out of newspaper already.

Clancy's scratch at the door interrupted his musings. Dek let the pair back inside.

At Misty Hills, Sarah looked across the breakfast table with concern.

Pale, drawn, and still in her robe, Raine sat listlessly rearranging scrambled eggs on her plate with a fork. Her disheveled hair hung limp and dull as she tucked a strand of it behind one ear.

"Did you look outside?" Sarah asked.

"Hm?" Raine cut her eyes to the window and back. "Oh, yeah. Nice." She nibbled a corner of toast, then put it down again. Pushing the plate away, she rose and took her things to the sink.

"I don't suppose you've any plans for today," Sarah said, probing gingerly into Raine's dark mood.

"No," she stated. "Not now, not ever."

"Oh, come on, old girl. Surely it's not the end of the world," Sarah said encouragingly. "I've been invited to go for a drive in a little while. Could you be persuaded to come along?"

Raine rubbed at her throbbing temples, suddenly recalling that Sarah had gone out with Steve the night before. "Oh. I'm sorry. I'd completely forgotten about your date. How was it?"

"I'm sure you've got too many things on your mind to listen to my prattle."

Taking her chair again, Raine forced a smile. "Nevertheless, I really am interested in my best friend. Tell me all about it." Resting her elbows on the table, she leaned forward.

"Sure you won't be bored?" Sarah appeared barely able to contain her excitement.

"No. Really. I want to know everything." Knowing her friend would hold back a bit out of sensitivity, Raine nevertheless tried hard to inure herself against hearing about someone else's happiness when her own dreams lay in ashes.

"Steve took me around Red Deer, showing me the historical sights," Sarah began, "then we ate at a lovely Chinese restaurant. We've ever so much to talk about. He's quite easy to be with."

Raine's expression brightened. "I figured you two would hit it off."

"I might say he's quite the nicest young man I've ever met."

"Wow, that's something to hear after a long list of crushes," Raine teased.

Sarah grimaced as a flush crept over her cheeks. "I know. I hardly believe it myself. But he's just so—so different. Settled, confident—"

"Handsome?" Raine cut in.

"He is that. Somehow I feel as though I've been searching for him all my life."

"Well," Raine said, with as much of a smile as she could manage, "this is beginning to sound serious."

Sarah nodded. "It might very well be. He's coming to see me again today. Wouldn't you like to come out with us for a little while? Get your mind on other things? We wouldn't want to desert you when you're hurting so."

Reaching across the space between them, Raine squeezed her hand. "It's really nice of you to ask. I appreciate it, truly. But I think I'd rather stay home. I haven't even taken my shower yet."

"Were you, um, able to get any sleep at all, last night?" Sarah asked gently.

Raine considered the question. Sleep? What was that? She averted her gaze, momentarily lost in bittersweet thoughts of yesterday. Her own slow intake of breath brought her back to the present, and she noticed that Sarah still awaited an answer. "Oh, I'm sure I must have dropped off once or twice."

"Well, as they say," came her friend's over-bright but

practical answer, "today's another day, and all that rubbish. Perhaps the pain will ease with time."

With a small huff, Raine shook her head. "I wonder who on earth came up with that piece of brilliance. Wouldn't it be wonderful if it really were true?" Rising, she pulled the belt of her robe tighter. "I'd better hit the shower. Have a nice time with Steve."

Later that week, after coming home from a trip into town, Lucas kicked off his boots in the entry and carried the groceries inside. He saw Raine curled up on the sitting room couch, half-heartedly working on a sketch. She closed the tablet and came to help.

"Sarah's out again, I presume?" he asked, watching Raine remove items from one of the bags and absently set them on the counter.

"Mm hm."

"That makes every day this week."

"I know."

Lucas frowned. "From the way you've been acting lately, I can't help but wonder about something. Are you by any chance sorry Sarah's here—especially now that she seems to have set her cap for your boyfriend?"

"What?" Raine's head snapped up. Normally she'd have found such an absurd idea humorous, only she didn't feel much like laughing just now. Instead, she sighed. "Daddy.

"Oh, I know you don't like to admit it, but—"

"Daddy," she said in a stronger tone. "No matter how much you might have wished it, Steven was never my boyfriend. He's really not my type at all."

"But you went out a couple times." His dear face was so puzzled that it looked almost comical.

Raine closed her eyes in frustration for a split second. "Yes, and it was a pleasant diversion for both of us. But we're barely even good friends. He and Sarah obviously hit it off right from the beginning, and she's in seventh heaven about it."

"And that's okay with you?"

"Yes. I'm very happy for them both."

A few lines furrowed her father's brow. "Then what else is wrong? You've hardly eaten a bite for days. There are dark circles under your eyes. You don't smile. You don't want to go anywhere, do anything—"

"It's nothing." *Nothing at all,* her thoughts continued. She was just dead inside. Turning her attention back to the groceries, she finished putting them away.

Neither spoke for several minutes, until her father broke the silence.

"When Sarah leaves, would you like to return to Haiti with her for a week or two? Maybe check in on Mark and Ruth, see how they are, take them a few things?"

Raine shook her head. "I don't think so. Anyway, I'll be surprised if Sarah even decides to go back, if you really want to know."

Her father rubbed his chin in thought, then looked over the frames of his glasses at her. "Hm. For some reason, I never gave that possibility any thought. If you're right, I don't think it'll set well with her mom and dad. They're probably still counting on her help at the clinic." He paused. "But on the other hand, I wouldn't be too happy sending *you* back into that mess, even for a short time. It's hard enough having Mark and his wife there. Who knows? Maybe Sarah's folks feel the same way." Reaching for the coffee pot, he poured leftover coffee into a mug and put it into the microwave.

That afternoon Raine went out to the barn for a welcome

reprieve from her father's constant hovering. She knew he was worried as much over her welfare now as he was about her brother's. She watched him perusing the daily newspapers every morning for the latest update on the political upheaval in Haiti before retiring to his bedroom to spend hours in prayer. She'd just have to convince him he didn't really need to fret about her. She'd be all right.

The stalls already had sufficient fresh straw, she noticed, giving them a quick once over, but she added a little more anyway, spreading it evenly with the hay fork. Storm nickered and nuzzled against her. She took two carrots from her pocket and gave one to him and the other to Buckwheat. One of these days she and Sarah should take them out for another long ride.

A tiny yip carried from an enclosed pen on the end, one normally vacant.

Her heart in her throat, Raine hesitated, fearing that some sort of wild animal had gotten into the barn. But a second yip, one much more playful, followed.

Cautiously she moved near enough to peer into the enclosure. Her mouth fell open. "Ohh," she whispered, immediately opening the pen and scooping up the mound of reddish fur. "Hello, puppy. How'd you get here? Where's—" Raine hugged the pup to herself and went to the door, looking from side to side for Dek. He was nowhere in sight. A heavy weight descended upon her. Surely she hadn't expected to see him.

She carried the animal back to the stall where she'd found it. In the corner sat a sturdy oval dog bed obviously built by loving hands. Stooping, she ran her fingers over the cool patina of the walnut finish and admired the smooth feel of it. A trace of the pup's warmth still clung to the fluffy blanket. Beside the bed sat a bag of puppy food and the book on dog care.

Raine shook her head in wonder and searched the remainder of the immediate area. No note. Not even a sign that Dek had been here. She sighed. She didn't deserve to have this sweet puppy, not after the way she'd fled from Dek a week ago, leaving him to think heaven knows what horrible things about her. Yet how like him to have entrusted her with its care anyway. Sinking down to her knees, she hugged the animal, then set it down and watched it take an old, worn rubber ball from a fold in the blanket and begin to play. But her thoughts were far down the lane, in a place she could never go again.

Dek crouched behind a stand of evergreens near the Montrose barn. Hat perched low on his forehead, he adjusted his scarf more snugly over his scars to keep out the stinging cold and rubbed his gloved hands together. What was taking Raine so long? He had waited what seemed like forever for her to come out to the barn. And now she'd been in there for ages.

Finally she emerged from the weathered structure, her arms full of squirmy puppy, and walked toward the house.

Dek steeled himself against the first flicker of warmth which flowed through him at the sight of her. After all, she'd made it more than plain that he no longer held any appeal whatsoever for her. But he couldn't stop the slow smile which crept over his mouth. They looked right together, the two redheads. The critter had grown a bit in the last few days and was real cute. By summer Raine would have a real companion. Not that it mattered to him at all. He just didn't have a use for two dogs.

As the door closed behind her, he stood, brushed himself off and trudged home. No way would he think about how silky her hair had looked blowing free above her down jacket.

Or how lovely the expression on her face had been as she kissed the pup with those flower soft lips. Somehow those things seemed incongruous with such a hard, cold heart. It wouldn't surprise him if she ended up taking the little dog to the pound.

In the house, Raine's father put down his book and reading glasses and bolted upright in the recliner as she approached carrying the puppy.

"What on earth—"

"Isn't she beautiful, Daddy?" Proudly, Raine set the playful mutt on the braided rug in the sitting room. It cocked its head, then bounded over to her father and nipped at his slippers.

"Where'd it come from?" he asked, scratching the velvety chin. He watched the puppy explore the fixtures of the room, sniffing things of apparent interest. It pranced back to Raine and licked her hand.

Raine felt her cheeks flame. "Um, she, uh, was a gift."

"Oh? I didn't know anyone in the area was breeding setters."

"No. She came from Banff." Inhaling for courage, Raine Confessed. "Dek was there a week or so ago and brought her back. He thought I should have some protection when I'm out drawing in the wilds."

"I see. Why didn't you ask him in?"

"He, um, couldn't stay," she blurted, cursing the blush that accompanied the lie. "Think I'll get the puppy a bowl of milk."

Lucas observed her quick exit and listened to her overly cheerful chatter as she fussed about in the kitchen. This Dek of hers certainly must be an odd character, coming by out of the blue bearing gifts, then vanishing an instant later. Nevertheless, it was good to see that light in Raine's eyes again. She had looked like a ghost the past several days, and often he'd heard her crying during the night when she thought everyone else was asleep. Maybe it had something to do with that young man.

Lucas couldn't bring himself to pry into his daughter's melancholy. She was of age, and when she wanted to talk he'd listen. But in the meantime someone must know something about the fellow. It was a pretty fair day for a walk to the neighboring farm. Perhaps while he was out he'd happen by Jim Wilcox's for some of that great coffee his wife, Bernice, kept on the stove. And ask a few casual questions.

After her father had gone for his walk, Raine put the finishing touches to her mother's portrait and stared longingly at the warm, loving face before closing the sketchbook. With Christmas rapidly approaching, she'd better start looking for a nice frame. She hoped her father would be surprised.

Beside her, the puppy slumbered in the special bed, which Raine had lugged inside while she had the house to herself. All curled up, the dog's round tummy rose and fell in even cadence with its breathing. She smiled. Such a pretty animal should have a name that did it justice.

Just then the door opened, and Sarah glided in.

Raine groaned inwardly and braced herself for the sight of her friend's glowing face. How could there still be any joy in this world, when she herself was so miserable?

Catching sight of Raine, Sarah stopped. "Oh. It was so quiet I thought perhaps no one was at home."

"No one is, except me," Raine said, noting that Sarah made an effort to subdue her bright smile—and even looked concerned.

"I must say you look a bit more chipper. Feeling better?"

Sarah asked.

"A bit. After all, one of us is happy, right?" She couldn't resist the barb.

An embarrassed glow covered Sarah's cheeks.

"Sorry," Raine mumbled with a helpless shrug. "I shouldn't blame you for my troubles. Come here. I have something to show you."

Sarah slipped off her coat and draped it over an arm as she crossed the room.

Raine pointed to the bed in the corner and waited for her friend's reaction.

"Oh. How very delightful." Scrunching down to the floor, Sarah curled her legs beneath her and studied the sleeping pile of fur. "Is this—"

"Yes. From Dek."

"You've seen him, then?" she asked hopefully. "Spoken to him?"

Raine sighed. "No. He just left the puppy in the barn. I found her when I went out there."

"Oh." The word came out on a disappointed note. "How very odd. But, surely he can't exactly hate you, then, since he quite obviously wants you to have the little dog. Don't you agree?"

"I don't really know what to think."

Sarah looked back at the animal, and her lips curved into a smile. She turned to Raine. "She's quite the treasure. What shall you call her?"

"I haven't decided. I wanted something that sounded Irish. Like Erin or Shannon. Or maybe a spice," she added almost as an afterthought. "What do you think of Cinnamon?"

Sarah considered the choice as she stared at the puppy. "Splendid. A jolly name for a jolly lass."

The comment pleased Raine, and suddenly she felt guilty for having been so wrapped up in herself—and thankful that Sarah was there. "How was your day? Or do I even need to ask?" she teased.

Sarah smiled coyly as she got up and took a seat beside her on the couch, her coat like a thick muff over her arms. "I don't know how to say this, or even if I should."

"What's that?" She dreaded hearing the answer.

"I . . . think I'm in love."

Raine felt a momentary flicker of jealousy and doused it at once with sheer determination. "I can't exactly say I'm surprised."

"Well *I* am. I'm almost afraid to believe it." Sarah's features clouded as she looked away. "Steven's asked me to stay on in Canada for awhile. See if we want to continue pursuing the relationship." Her gaze softened as she leaned her head back and stared up at the ceiling.

Watching her for a few seconds, Raine tried not to be envious. Only a few short days ago, she herself had held the fragile promise of love in her fingers for a tiny space of time. Since then, there had been moments when she had seriously considered paying whatever price it required just to have that precious feeling back. But in her saner moments, she knew she could not. A vow was a vow. She closed her eyes against the pain that intensified within her. Drawing a deep breath, she let it out slowly. "I think you should stay."

Sarah raised her head. "Do you?"

Raine nodded.

"If I do, I'll secure a flat of my own, or something. I couldn't impose upon you and your father indefinitely."

"Why not? We have plenty of room. I like having you around. Even if you *are* disgustingly happy," she added wryly.

With an understanding smirk, Sarah reached over and gave her a hug. "I never meant for this to happen. I feel dreadful knowing you're so sad. But I shall think about what to do." Her brows rose in lines of worry. "Wouldn't that be the shock of the century to Mum and Dad? How would I even tell them? This has all happened so quickly, we've hardly had time to catch our breath."

Raine smiled with feigned enthusiasm. "Oh, sometimes things have a way of working out . . . . Someone told me that not too long ago."

Sarah's light laugh brought an answering one from Raine.

In the corner, a sleepy Cinnamon stirred and stretched. Climbing out of bed, the little dog meandered a few feet away and assumed an all-too-familiar position.

Raine jumped up. "Oh, no you don't!" Grabbing the pup, she carried it gingerly outside.

fifteen

Dek opened his Bible to the Gospel of Luke and read the familiar Christmas story, then compared it to the similar account in Matthew. What boundless love God had for the world, he marveled, to allow His innocent Son to die as a sacrifice for sin. He bowed his head and said a silent prayer of gratitude.

In the fireplace, a log snapped and broke with a hiss, sending a shower of sparks spiraling up the chimney. Startled from his slumber. O'Clancy gave a wide yawn punctuated by a squeal and resumed his nap beside the recliner.

Dek reached down and idly ruffled the dog's ears. "Not much of a holiday, is it, pal? But I didn't think you'd be much help putting up a tree." He smiled at the comical thought. "Who needs one anyway? Great. Now I'm talking to myself." With a frown, he shook his head and relaxed against the headrest, recalling times not so long past when Christmas had been special. There had been trees, decorations, lights, the succulent aroma of a fat turkey dressed and roasting in the oven, pies—and church services on Christmas Eve bringing a beautiful reminder of the unfolding of God's magnificent plan.

The season had been fun in so many ways back then. Back when he knew the joy of tucking a secret present into a stocking, of having other unexpected and thoughtful ones awaiting someone's shining eyes. Christmas was a time for love, for laughter. For sharing memories with a very special person. He'd had someone, once, he reminded himself, and

169

had come pretty close a second time. Grimly he dismissed the memory of Raine as quickly as it surfaced. He wondered how thick the scar tissue on his charred heart would have to be before he could think about her without hurting.

His eyes explored the barren mantel and the equally bleak room. If it hadn't been for the calendar in the kitchen, he might have forgotten tomorrow would be December twenty-fifth.

In desperation he got up and crossed to the stereo. He had no holiday music among the collection of compact discs he'd acquired since the fire, but there'd be a good variety of carols on the FM, he was sure.

As the cheery notes of "Deck the Halls" filled the house, he brightened and looked at Clancy. "I'll bet Grace is already whipping up the dressing for a big old tom to be popped into the oven. Wanna go for a ride?"

Despite her melancholy on Christmas morning, the sight of brightly wrapped gifts around the tree lifted Raine's spirits, she clenched her hands in her lap and watched her dad peel off the wrappings of the special one from her.

His face took on an expression of utter amazement, "Oh," he gasped. "Honey." Taking out the charcoal portrait, he gazed at it lovingly, then looked up. "Did you do this?"

She nodded.

"It's . . . why, it's wonderful." He lightly stroked the beloved cheek of his wife in the sketch as his eyes grew misty. "I had no idea you possessed such talent." He got up and gave her a hug.

"I'm glad you like it, Daddy. I did have a little help." Immediately, Raine wished she had bitten her tongue.

Unbidden thoughts rushed forth to fill her with a sad longing. She felt herself tremble.

"That Dek of yours?" her dad asked pleasantly.

Raine could only muster a weak smile.

"Well. I'm quite impressed. I'm looking forward to meeting him soon."

Not in this lifetime, or even the next, Raine thought miserably.

Admiring the portrait once more, her dad set it aside and bent to pick up a long, narrow package. "This is for you. Merry Christmas, honey."

She forced some enthusiasm and knelt to unwrap it, trying to imagine what might be under the festive paper and ribbon. As she tore away the outer covering, she read the words on the box with a smile of surprise. "Ohh, Daddy. A portable stool!"

He grinned. "Well, since you're an artist, I thought you should have some of the proper equipment. It folds up nice and compact. Wait and see." Taking out his pocket knife, he undid the heavy duty staples in the box, then opened the end flaps while she pulled out the little seat.

"I just love it. Love it!" Jumping up, she hugged him.

"Hey," came Sarah's voice as she approached with a yawn, drawing the belt of her purple velvet robe tighter. "What's all the commotion out here?"

Raine met her friend's sleepy eyes. "We got tired of waiting for you to decide to join the world of the living, that's all."

Sarah gave an embarrassed shrug.

"Yes," Raine's father piped in. "We each opened a present. Let's see if I can find one with your name on it before we have breakfast."

Endless weeks passed in dull sameness as winter reluctantly released its grip on the countryside. The temperature inched upward, and patches of dismal snow diminished in number and size as the first tentative shoots of spring pushed fragile fingers up through the hard ground.

Raine had not seen Dek since the day she'd fled his place in tears, but he was never far from her thoughts. Whenever she went up on the gravel road to collect the mail, she would peer toward the stream and his cabin, but the futile effort always brought a sigh of disappointment.

"Didn't you say you'd had a driving lesson not long ago?" Sarah asked one morning as she sprinkled sugar onto her oatmeal.

Her question broke into Raine's daydreams at the kitchen sink. She stopped washing the few breakfast things and turned. "Yes, just before you came. Why?"

"Well, I'm sure even you must be getting weary of moping around here all the time," Sarah chided gently. "I thought perhaps now that the season has begun to change you might consider getting in some more practice."

Raine smiled and took a deep breath. "You know, that's not a half bad idea. There are plenty of access roads on the property, and the ground is drying quickly."

"And," her friend continued, "one of these days when your father has errands to run, you could go with him and pick up a driving permit. With summer on the way you might enjoy having the freedom to go somewhere on your own."

Raine mulled over Sarah's words. The suggestion was very convincing. Several magnificent parks were within a reasonable distance. How wonderful it would be to drive the breathtaking David Thompson Highway, to sketch mountains and waterfalls, emerald lakes and glaciers known the world over for their beauty. It had been ages since she'd done any new drawings, and a change of scenery would work wonders on her hibernating spirit. "Want to come with me while I take the car out?" she asked.

"Can't, thanks. Other plans."

"Now, why does that not surprise me?" Raine teased. "Good thing we get to see one another most mornings, huh?"

Sarah's expression remained blank as nonchalantly she eased her placemat out from under her cereal bowl and threw it at Raine, hitting her shoulder.

Raine giggled and turned back to her chore, wishing for a tiny second that she and her friend were still at boarding school, carefree and always on the lookout for fun. But those days had passed forever. Sarah now wore a diamond on her left hand and had a collection of bridal magazines to furnish ideas for a perfect wedding. Raine sighed. Her own life was pathetic. Other than watching rapidly growing Cinnamon's playful antics, days dragged by in slow motion, each a carbon copy of the one before. "Think I'll go get Daddy's keys," she said, drying her hands.

Once she took the car out, Raine discovered with relief that it didn't take long to get accustomed to the clutch again. Dek had been a good teacher. She allowed herself a few bittersweet memories of her first driving lesson as she shifted gear and passed the barn and outbuildings. Near one of the cattle ponds on the way to the open pasture she stopped and feasted her eyes. Rows and rows of faraway watercolor hills lent a soft backdrop to the ranch. How could she have stayed inside for so long? With spring's first kiss upon the winter-weary landscape, Raine ached to get back into her art again.

After lunch, Raine saddled Storm and rode partway down the lane. Cinnamon scampered alongside, stopping to explore various points of interest and then racing in boundless puppy energy to catch up. Sparing herself the sight of Dek's cabin, Raine angled westward, hoping to come across an appealing portion of the creek.

When she came to a bend in the water flanked by clusters of birch and tamarack, she took out the viewfinder Dek had given her and peered through it until she settled upon a satisfactory angle. Then, swinging off the horse, she unfastened her stool and sat down with her sketchbook, lightly roughing in the preliminary outlines.

Cinnamon sniffed Raine's boots, then meandered nearby, poking her wet little nose into the nooks and crannies of trees and rocks. Finally she returned to Raine's side and sat panting till her liquidy chocolate eyes grew heavy. She curled up in a puddle of sunlight.

The sleeping pup provided inspiration for a second sketch. Already she had nearly doubled in size. Soon her beautiful coat would be as long and silky as O'Clancy's. With a sigh, Raine straightened to ease a few kinks in her back and turned to a clean page.

Working in the blissful quiet, Raine reflected upon two familiar verses from Psalm thirty-seven, which she had read in her morning devotions:

> *Delight yourself in the Lord and he will give you the desires of your heart . . . .*
> *The Lord delights in the way of the man whose steps he has made firm; though he stumble, he will not fall, for the Lord upholds him with his hand.*

Realizing what exactly made up the desires of her heart, Raine felt the warmth of a blush and stopped sketching as a guilty smile broke free. She ventured a useless glance in the direction of Dek's place. She missed seeing him. If only . . . . *Now don't start that,* an inner voice warned. *Concentrate on what you're doing.*

A red-winged blackbird flitted about in the treetops, then flew away with his speckled lady-friend, emitting a rich musical O-ka-LEEE!

Cinnamon stirred and opened her eyes. Tipping her head comically at Raine, she got up with an elaborate stretch, then pranced in a few circles. When a noise came through the bushes nearby, she took off after it.

Used to seeing rabbits and field mice in her travels, Raine absently watched Cinnamon pursue an indefinable woodland animal ambling away toward the trees. Just as the creature reached the nearest tree the pup's frame blocked Raine's view.

Cinnamon yelped in pain and jumped backward.

Raine sprang up. A feeling of dread cinched her heart at the sight of the puppy running crazily to her, whimpering and whining. It stopped once to swipe at its nose with a paw, then shook its head in wild confusion.

As Raine scooped Cinnamon up to comfort her, she saw a handful of wicked-looking porcupine quills sticking out of Cinnamon's snout and nose. "You're hurt!" she cried. "Oh, you poor baby." A sinking fear flashed into her mind that the quills could be lethal to young dogs—or at the very least, cause an infection. Frantically she sought her bearings. The ranch was out of reach, but Dek's cabin was not far downstream. Without another thought, she loosened

Storm's reins and led the horse along as she carried Cinnamon in her arms. *Please let Dek be there, Lord,* she begged.

"Dek!" She yelled as she neared his land. "Dek! Help me! Please help!"

Almost instantly Dek's door jerked open. He took the steps in one leap and raced toward her. "What happened?" His gaze fell upon the whimpering pup.

"Cinnamon's hurt," Raine wailed. "What should I do?"

Dek lay a hand on her shoulder and squeezed. "First of all, calm down," he said gently as he took the animal. "I'll take her inside while you tether the horse. Then come in. I'll need some help."

"W . . . will she be okay?" Raine asked in a small voice.

"She'll be fine. I promise."

His words did much to soothe her jangled nerves. Drying her face with the back of her hand, Raine fastened Storm's reins to a branch and hurried inside.

"I'm in the basement," Dek called as the door slammed behind her. Following the direction of his voice, Raine went to the stairs, barely noticing his efficient and functional workshop as she descended.

"This is not going to be pleasant, so call up some of that nurse's training of yours while we do what has to be done." He placed the dog back into her arms and crossed to the other end of the room. "I'll try to be as careful as I can."

Feeling trembly herself, Raine marveled at Cinnamon's calm, at her trusting eyes. The only evidence of fear came from the little staccato heartbeats Raine could feel through her jacket sleeves. She swallowed. "What can I do?"

Dek returned from his toolbox holding a pair of pliers. Raine felt all the color drain from her face.

He gave an encouraging nod. "I need you to hold her real

still for me."

This was beyond her worst imaginings. Raine's heart plummeted as she realized how a parent must feel when its own flesh and blood has been hurt.

"Ready?" Dek asked.

She nodded and hugged Cinnamon against herself.

One by one, a yank of the pliers dislodged a cruel barb and drew blood. And with each pitiful puppy cry, shards of pain pierced Raine's own heart. When the last one came out, she buried her face in the dog's fur and wept softly. "I'm so sorry," she whispered.

Dek patted her shoulder. "You did great. And this was not your fault. Most young dogs have to suffer through a few valuable lessons when they live in the bush country. She will never go near a porcupine again. I'll show you." Reaching to the table at his elbow, he picked up a barbed quill and held it to Cinnamon's nose.

The dog whimpered and shied closer to Raine.

"See?"

With a shudder, Raine grimaced. "Still, I could have been more careful while I was drawing. I should have been watching out for her."

"Hey," Dek smiled. "She's the one who's going to be watching out. From now on, she'll be a bit wary while she's enjoying the great outdoors. And she'll let *you* know when there's danger." He poured antiseptic on a cotton ball and dabbed the pup's sore nose. "All done. A bowl of milk and a treat, and she'll be almost as good as new." He stroked the coppery head good-naturedly, rubbing behind the dog's floppy ears. He was rewarded with a lick on his hand.

"Will she get sick or anything?" Raine asked.

"Not likely. She's had her shots, right? There shouldn't

be a problem. Come on upstairs." Turning, he started up the steps with Clancy at his heels.

"Thank you, Dek," she said, releasing Cinnamon and watching her scurry after the other dog. "I really appreciate this."

"Any friend would have done the same," he called back.

Raine brushed off the front of her jacket and wiped her face with a tissue from her pocket before mounting the stairs. She found the dogs happily lapping bowls of milk in the kitchen. Crossing to the sink, she washed her hands and face, then dried them on a hand towel. She felt Dek's presence before he spoke.

"Could I offer you some hot chocolate while—Cinnamon, is it—recuperates?"

She turned. "That would be nice." Dek's hopeful smile stabbed at her heart. He looked older. Tired. And she noticed he again kept only his good side toward her.

Gesturing toward the kitchen chairs, he went to the cupboard.

Taking a seat, Raine watched her pup for several moments to be certain everything seemed okay, then transferred her attention to the stove as Dek scooped cocoa from a can into a pot and added milk. Her gaze swept over several books lying across the table, and her breathing stopped. An open *Bible*. A commentary and assorted study guides—an impressive selection of them for a man supposedly not interested in spiritual matters. What could it mean? Her heart tripped over itself as she craned her neck and saw that the passage he'd been working on was in Psalm thirty-four. He had underlined several of the verses, including the ones which had come to mind while she was drawing. Wondering if he'd been trying to prove—or disprove—something, she contemplated how to bring up the subject.

"Sorry for the clutter," Dek said, removing the books and putting them on the counter. He took two mugs from a stand and filled them. "So, how have you been?"

"Fine, thanks. And you?" She shifted in her seat.

"The same. The pup looks great. Has she been good for you?"

"Yes. Very."

"I'm glad. I wondered." Returning with the cups, he placed one before Raine, then took a seat. "Sorry I don't have any sweets to offer you. I don't normally keep them around."

"I know." Raine smiled to herself. She scanned the titles in the pile of study books and opened her mouth to ask about them, but not quickly enough.

"It's . . . good to see you," he said softly.

Raine met his eyes. They seemed a shade darker than she remembered and held hers for a breathless moment.

"I've always wished I had apologized for—well, you know, he began, lifting a hand helplessly.

She took a sip of the rich chocolate and set down the mug. "Please don't. There's nothing you have to be sorry for."

"How can you say that?" he asked, emitting a whoosh of breath. "The trail of dust you left didn't settle for days."

Unable to stop herself, Raine smiled. How she had missed his wit. But the humor evaporated when he spoke again.

"I knew the boundaries. You said in the beginning that you needed a friend. I overstepped."

"Please, Dek." She put a hand to her temples and closed her eyes for a brief second. "I can't talk about this right now. My insides are in shreds after the ordeal downstairs. I can't deal with anything else heavy just yet."

"Then when *could* you, Raine, if you don't mind my asking?"

His appeal, soft, sensible, cut through her like a knife. Feeling uneasy over her own part in their separation, she could not answer.

"Well, anyway," he said, "I'm sorry. For everything. I won't bring it up again."

Neither spoke for a long moment. Raine took another swallow, and her gaze wandered once more to his Bible on the counter. Drawing a fortifying breath, she ventured a look in his direction. All the normal animation was missing in his wooden expression. His eyes appeared glazed, dull, far away. She cleared her throat, and he glanced up. "Are you, um, studying anything interesting?" she asked, almost fearful of his answer.

Dek followed her line of vision and shrugged. "*I* think so." He debated about elaborating, but decided something else was more pressing. "Actually, I have a confession to make, and I might as well get it over with while I have this chance."

A look of puzzlement came to her face.

"I had no right to take my spiritual frustrations out on you when we first met. It had nothing to do with you. It was between God and me."

"Was?" The word was little more than a whisper.

"Yes." Self-conscious, suddenly, Dek nearly changed his mind, but reason prevailed. This would probably be the last time he would ever see her. If nothing else, she might at least appreciate the fact that the Lord had answered a few of her prayers for a *friend*. He formulated his reply. "Not too long ago I decided to stop running. From God, I mean.

Some things happened, and I had some time to think."

She blinked, then stared at him with those incredible green eyes.

Dek wondered if the glow in them had always been there or had just intensified. In any case he felt as though she could see right into his soul, that she'd always possessed that ability. He shifted in his chair and hunkered down a little into his collar.

"What did you say?" she asked.

He laughed, and it put him more at ease. "Don't tell me you didn't have any faith in all those prayers you and everyone else I know in the world have been saying for me," he said incredulously with a half-smile. "That *is* unbelievable."

"I—"

"Not that I'd really gotten all that far in the first place, with the Lord gripping my suspenders, you understand," he continued.

"What do you mean?"

Dek grinned, a little embarrassed. "I had accepted Him as my Savior back in my teens. So even though I tried to go my own stubborn way after the fire, He kept sending people across my path who let me know they were praying for me. You happened to be one of them, by the way, and I want you to know I appreciated it."

Raine could not think of a response as his words slowly made their way into her brain.

"Anyway," Dek went on, "one night in frustration I unloaded all my bitterness into God's lap. Told Him everything I'd been thinking and feeling and had kept bottled up inside like a cancer." He rolled his eyes and shook his head. "Just hearing that stuff coming out of my mouth was enough for me to realize how I'd been wallowing in self-pity for the last few years. I finally asked the Lord to forgive me for all the time I wasted running from Him." His fingers absently brushed through his curly hair. "And He took me back."

"I can't believe what I'm hearing," Raine said. "It's so—

Dek gave a sheepish grin. "It was bound to happen sooner or later. There's no defense against the power of prayer, you know. And I guess that's fortunate for a lot of people. Was for me, at any rate."

Cinnamon and O'Clancy tumbled over Dek's boot just then and started running a playful lap around the table. One sharp whistle, and the larger dog skidded to a stop. "Come on, you guys," he said, getting up. He let them out the back door. "Would you like to go in and sit where it's more comfortable?" he said, motioning toward the parlor.

Raine wasn't positive she could trust her legs at this point, but she smiled and rose, aware that he followed closely as they went into the next room. She sank onto the leather couch and watched Dek walk to the window and put his hands in the back pockets of his jeans, looking out.

Never in her wildest dreams had she actually expected anything so near the desires of her heart! When she had told him goodbye, it had been a final parting, one of obedience. Now to hear that he, too, belonged to the Lord, to consider the possibility that God Himself had bridged the gulf that had separated them . . . . Glorious joy flowed through her being. She was afraid to speak, for fear she was reading more into it than there really was.

Dek waited for Raine to say something. Anything. But as he stared outside, he heard no comment from her. He breathed a prayer that things would somehow be all right again between them. Then as soon as he asked that, he amended it to just having her in his life, however she would come. As a friend, if that was all he could have. An art student—he'd settle for even that if he had to. Just don't let her say goodbye again for good. He'd never be able to stand that. Not after she had made him come back to life. Please don't leave me again, Raine, his heart pleaded.

His gaze fell upon his ravaged hand, and a heaviness descended upon his chest, pressing all the breath out of him, crushing the last remnants of hope. He would always be scarred. Grotesque. She'd always be ashamed of him. The hard chunk of reality sank inside his heart and hit bottom. He gave a deep sigh as his shoulders slumped with the finality of it all. Forcing himself to raise his head, he worked up nerve enough to glance her way, to memorize the tip of her head, the color of her hair. There'd be a million empty nights he would have to call them to his memory just to survive.

But when he turned, he found Raine right behind him.

"I . . . I don't know what to say," she breathed. "To know that you have made peace again with God . . . . I should have known it when I looked into your eyes."

He made a wry grimace in a futile attempt to keep things light, trying to keep her from saying it was time to go. He wanted his heart to drink in the sound of her voice one last time. "What chance did I have anyway?" he teased. "You weren't content to let me stay comfortable in my misery."

"No. Nor will I ever again," she said. "I promise."

Dek wasn't altogether sure he'd heard right. But her lips were curved in a wondrous smile, and those emerald eyes were beckoning, inviting, as she softly slipped her hand inside his scarred one and lifted it to her lips. For a minute he forgot how to breathe. He opened his arms, and with a joyous sound, she moved into them. He drew her close and buried his face in her silky red hair. "When you came today, I was positive it was the last time I would ever see you. That when you left . . . ."

Raine pressed closer and tightened her arms around him. "It crossed my mind too," she confessed. "But right now I'm convinced that the Lord brought me here, that He wanted us to have this day."

"I only hope you're right." Dek cupped the back of his head and looked heavenward, breathing a prayer of thankfulness as he held her close. "You . . . deserve someone more . . . acceptable than I am," he said huskily, surprised that he'd spoken the words aloud.

She lifted a radiant smile. "Oh, you mean because of this?" she said, sliding her fingers ever so gently upward over his left cheek. "I wouldn't trade this perfect face for a thousand others. You don't ever have to hide from me." Rising to tiptoe, she softly kissed the scars.

Dek almost flinched. He felt a stinging behind his eyes and closed them for a heartbeat. No one but medical attendants at the burn center had touched his face for years. As Raine curved her palm over it, her touch, soft as a gossamer angel wing, stole his breath away.

"It has to do with viewpoint, you know."

"Viewpoint?" he echoed.

"All I see when I look at you is beauty," she said, "reflections of the man you are, shining out of your heart."

"You mean you really don't care about my scars? That's not why you ran away that day?"

Raine's green eyes blurred in a mist of tears. "I would really hate having you think me capable of something that shallow, Alan Decker," she teased, then grew serious and looked straight at him. "It had to do with a vow I had made to God, that I would not seek a relationship with someone who didn't feel as strongly about Him as I do. It was an act of obedience, and losing you was like having a part of myself amputated. I wanted to die."

"Knowing how much your faith means to you, I can understand that," he said. "I really can." Dek held her tight for several minutes, until he could trust himself to speak. "I love you, Raine Montrose. I have from that day on the porch when you plied me with brownies and dared me to open my door."

"And I have loved you since that night you rode up on your shining black horse and rescued me," she answered. Her lips parted in a sweet smile, and he lowered his to them. She tasted of chocolate and sweet yesterdays, and answered his kiss with tender promises of tomorrows and forever.

Having Raine in his arms once again, exquisite and soft, Dek had to use every ounce of strength he had—and some he didn't know existed—to ease her away. He wasn't altogether sure he could trust himself for much longer. He planted a kiss on her lightly freckled nose. "I . . . think you and Cinnamon had better go now," he said on a shaky breath.

"Yes. I know." But instead she slid her arms around his waist, snuggling close. "Would you come with me? There's someone I want very much for you to meet . . . just in case there's something special you might want to ask him."

Dek chuckled. He brushed a wisp of hair from her eyes and ran a finger lightly over the curve of her cheek. "Sure. I'll go saddle my horse. There *is* something special I want to ask *you* on the way home." He drew Raine into his embrace once more, thankful that at last he'd stopped running, that he had finally come home himself.

Home. It was a beautiful word.

A Letter To Our Readers

Dear Readers:

In order that we might better contribute to your reading enjoyment, we would appreciate your taking a few minutes to respond to the following questions and return to:

Editor
Heartsong Presents
P.O. Box 719
Uhrichsville, Ohio 44683

1. Did you enjoy reading *Reflections of the Heart*?
   ❑ Very much. I would like to see more books by this author!
   ❑ Moderately
   ❑ I would have enjoyed it more if

   _____

2. Where did you purchase this book?_____

   _____

3. What influenced your decision to purchase this book?
   ❑ Cover   ❑ Back cover copy
   ❑ Title   ❑ Friends
   ❑ Publicity   ❑ Other _____

4. Please rate the following elements from 1 (poor) to 10 (superior).
   - ❏ Heroine ❏ Plot
   - ❏ Hero ❏ Inspirational theme
   - ❏ Setting ❏ Secondary characters

5. What settings would you like to see in Heartsong Presents Books?

   _____

   _____

6. What are some inspirational themes you would like to see treated in future books?

   _____

   _____

7. Would you be interested in reading other Heartsong Presents books?
   - ❏ Very interested
   - ❏ Moderately interested
   - ❏ Not interested

8. Please indicate your age:
   - ❏ Under 18 ❏ 25-34 ❏ 46-55
   - ❏ 18-24 ❏ 35-45 ❏ Over 55

Name _____

Occupation _____

Address _____

City _____ State _____ Zip _____